DEATH INVITES IN GOLD

RACHEL BROSS

PROLOGUE
SMALL TOWN USA, 2013, PODUNK HIGH

In the lunchroom, a girl sits hunched over a book, alone, at a table. Her scraggly red hair falls on either side of her face, obscuring her view of anything other than her book.

A hand reaches across the pages, slamming the book down on the table.

The girl locks onto bleach-blond dreads falling over the table. "Nathan, leave me alone." She glares at him, trying her best to pull the book from his grasp.

Nathan laughs, looking above her as her little decorative top hat falls from her head. He leans away, letting go of her book, and swats her hat farther across the table.

A mass of short black curls blocks the girl's view as a dark rosewood-skinned boy with brown eyes and a strong jaw lined with a less than mediocre beard leans against the table to her right. She huffs.

Grinning, the boy laughs. "Oops, sorry, Wonka, I mean Wanda." He offers his best and most charming white-toothed smile.

Wanda rolls her eyes, reaching for her hat.

A new hand swats it across the table towards Nathan. "Oh,

I'm sorry! I meant to grab it." A busty redhead sits at her left, covering her deep red lips with her fingertips.

Wanda rolls her eyes again, clinging to her book, and draws it closer to her. "Please leave me alone." Her words come out just above a whisper as she puts the book in her lap and reaches a hand towards the floor to her hat, so close yet so far away.

A designer sneaker pushes the hat into the space between tables. "Aww, c'mon, Wanda, don't you like us?" A light yet male voice carries over the rest, and he chuckles. "We're your friends." Long black hair falls over the table, leading to another strong, square jaw, charming smile, and tight-slit brown eyes.

Wanda white-knuckles the sides of her book in her lap, glaring at the table, and doesn't speak.

Before she can attempt to move away or get up, the rest of the pack descends. Six more students sit around the table. Five boys and five girls surround her now.

A cute, bubbly girl pulls at Wanda's vest. "Whatcha got so many buttons for? You look like a refrigerator!" She giggles, squishing her face up, and her short bleach-blond curls bob about her cheeks as she looks around the table.

The girl tugs at a red button with a set of parted lips on it.

Wanda swats her hand away. "They're movie buttons from my favorites." She rubs her fingers over the shining metal.

Nathan points his chin at her. "Yea, why's it a pair of chick's lips? You into girls or somethin'?" He snickers, licking his lips, and blows her a kiss.

The bubbly girl swats at him. "Ew, Nathan. Of course she's not." She cuts her eyes at Wanda. "Are you?" She holds her gaze, arching an eyebrow.

Wanda speaks just above a whisper. "No." She cuts her eyes around the table as they all pick at their food.

Nathan snickers. "Why're you so interested, Bubbles?" He smirks at her, cutting his eyes at her. "You interested in them?" He licks his lips, looking her over.

A petite Asian girl with a layered bob curving around a sneer tosses a bit of lettuce from her lunchroom salad at him. "Shut up, Nathan! I'm sure she gets enough pussy from Blake." She cuts her eyes at the boy with long black hair. "He's so pretty he might as well be a girl." She holds a stare, smirking, and leans into Hugh.

Blake slings his hair from his shoulder, crossing his arms, and glares at her.

The Asian girl snorts, shaking her head. "Proves my point."

Blake rolls his eyes. "Brenda, baby, please explain to her how satisfied you are with our relationship." He puts out a hand towards Miku.

Brenda giggles. "My Asian supersedes all Asians and gives me that tentacle all night long." She leans towards him, planting a huge kiss across the table.

Everyone *ohs* and *ughs*, leaning or turning away.

Wanda leans away, curling her fingers into her black hoodie. "Why're y'all over here anyway? We're not friends." She shrinks into herself, taking painstaking measures not to watch the interaction taking place so close to her.

The guys snigger, bumping and pushing each other.

A large and burly blond boy pushes Blake into the dark rosewood-skinned boy to Wanda's right, making her fall into the redhead on her left.

Wanda brushes her hair from her face, revealing a patch of red, pink, and purple discoloration around her right eye and down her cheek. Without thinking, she tucks the hair behind her ear, leaving her face uncovered as she scans the caf for free tables far away from them.

A tan guy with short black curls sitting directly across from Wanda next to Nathan drops his fork, grunting, and looks across the room to his left. "Ugh! Thanks, Jeb! Now I've lost my appetite because the freak uncovered her face." He points to Wanda.

Wanda returns her gaze to the table, letting her hair fall over her face again.

An alder-skinned girl sitting across the table swats at him. "Shut up, Tyler! Damn. She can't help it." She glances at Wanda, offering a weak grin.

Wanda just looks at the table, making her hair cover more of her face.

Tyler pushes his tray forward, crosses his arms, and glares at the black girl. "Fine, Dorine, if you're so cool with it, then why'd you make that face when you looked at it just now? Hm?" He smirks. "I agree with Wonka. Why are we over here when we don't even like her?" Running his tongue along the inside of his bottom lip, he looks around the table.

The dark-skinned boy chuckles, nudging Wanda's shoulder, making her shy away, and he cuts his eyes at Tyler. "C'mon, man, she ain't that bad." He turns to her, poking his chin out, and grins. "Are ya, Wonka?" Chuckling, he puts an arm around the Asian girl, cutting his eyes at her sweet and innocent-looking grin.

The Asian girl lets out a light giggle, cutting her eyes at Wanda. "Ya know, Hugh, I rather like her disfigurement." She smirks. "Gives her a fierce Japanese-looking edge." Her giggle returns. "They should turn her into a comic." He puts out a hand, moving it over with each word. "Red-Faced Shogun of Hell." She smirks again, putting her hand in her lap. "I can see her face plastered everywhere as the poster for a monster-killer." Her smirk never wavers as she meets Wanda's glare.

Hugh raises a finger from the Asian girl's shoulder. "Aw, Miku, that sounds badass." He shifts in his seat, adjusting his arm on her shoulder.

Miku grins at him.

Jeb stuffs a giant forkful of spaghetti into his mouth, letting the sauce redden his grizzly beard, and speaks with his mouth stuffed. "You guys gonna come to the game tonight? It's my last one of the year." He chomps, smacking, and looks back and forth between everyone and his food as he brings another giant forkful to his mouth.

A dirty-blond-haired girl with flawless makeup sitting beside him curls her lip a bit as she reaches for a napkin. "Ugh, Jeb, wipe your beard." She flips her perfectly teased hair over her shoulder, brushing French tips over her pristine cheer uniform top. "Y'all had better be there to help me cheer on my little Jebby." She cuts her eyes across the table. "He's gonna need all the pep we can give him if he's gonna get that scholarship and go pro." She smirks, sliding her hand over his thigh, and then scrunches her face when he turns to her.

For the first time since they all sat down, no one speaks for several seconds, and then Nathan shakes his head. "Nah, man, I've got some fish to catch if you know what I mean." He chuckles, glancing over at the red head, and winks.

The red head snarls, rolling her eyes, and crosses her arms as she looks off at the other end of the table. "In your dreams, Nathan." She snarls again.

Nathan laughs. "Oh, sweet Paulina, yes! You give the best head in my dreams." He laughs again, high-fiving Jeb across the table.

The table erupts into laughter.

All, that is, except Wanda, who shrinks farther and farther away until she's able to slip her legs off the seat and break away from them. Scooping up her hat, she speed-walks out of the caf.

CHAPTER ONE
THE BIG APPLE 2019, A SMALLTIME
NEWSPAPER COMPANY

Tyler, grown, buff, and charmingly handsome, sits behind a desk with an old Mac keyboard below his fingers and wiggles them above the designated typing starter keys. "C'mon, man, think of something to write." He sighs, staring at his fingers above the keys. "Damn it." He puts his hands over his face, turning in his desk chair, and grunts into his palms.

A knock comes from the open door.

Tyler lowers his hands enough to cut his eyes towards the door.

A petite young blonde pokes her head inside with an over-exaggerated grin that turns into a cringe. "I'm sorry! I know you didn't want to be disturbed, but they're hounding me." She clenches her teeth, wobbling her head, and glances at the ceiling, speaking through her teeth. "Uuugh..." Her gaze returns to him. "Do you have anything for me to give them?" She shifts around, pressing herself against the frame, and braces herself with a hand inside the room.

Tyler huffs, turning back to his desk, and crosses his arms over the edge. "No." He shakes his head, tousling his short black curls, and lets his hand swipe over his beard as it falls back to the desk. "The movie was crap, but I can't say that because apparently I'm 'too negative.'" He puts air quotes around the last two words. "I need this job. I need it to get to the one I want." He lays his head on his arm, rolling it a few times, and speaks towards the floor. "How should I bullshit this?" He keeps his head down and groans.

The blonde tiptoes her way into the closet of an office, glancing over her shoulder, and closes the door, talking low. "Well, was there anything you liked about it at all?" She inches her way closer to his desk, sitting on the corner, and adjusts her blouse.

Tyler speaks without raising his head. "No, everything about it was contrived and trite. The best part was the dog, and he dies." He looks up, opening his mouth to speak, and stops short, glaring at the pair of black-lace-covered breasts so close to his face.

The blonde pushes out her breasts, moving them from side to side as she speaks. "Maybe I can give you some... inspiration." She bites her bottom lip, letting it slide slowly from between her teeth.

Tyler sits straight, sliding his hands over his spread thighs, and licks his lips. "Yea, maybe you can." He smirks as she turns towards him with a smile.

The blonde undoes the rest of the buttons on her blouse, pulling the pair of chopsticks from her bun, and shakes her hair free. With a foot, she tucks her toes below the seat of his chair and pulls him towards her.

The wheels squeak and squeal as his weight moves over the floor.

Giggling, she spreads her legs, tugging at the hem of her black pencil skirt, and slides her foot between his legs all the way to his crotch.

Tyler breathes deep, looking her over, and then closes his eyes as her foot slips and moves over his hardening dick. "Come 'ere." Lurching forward, he picks her up from her perch, setting her in his lap.

The blonde lets out a quick squeal, settling her legs on either side of him, and leans her chest into his face.

———

Newport, RI

In a four-story mansion that has a rock circle driveway around a three-tier fountain and a tennis court and pool out back behind the courtyard:

A tall, daunting woman tromps across the grey marble flooring of the foyer, running her Swiffer duster over the Chinese vases amassed on each self.

Merrien saunters through, pink silk robe fluttering and billowing behind her. "Oh, Brunhilda! Do be a dear and clean out Fifi's doggy box. I can't stand the smell it gives off." She flicks the maid a smile, tapping and gently pushing at the overly large rollers in her designer-dyed hair.

Brunhilda mutters to herself in German as she continues to dust around highly delicate décor.

Merrien giggles, stopping short of the kitchen door. "Nehmen Sie diesen Ton nicht mit. Ich werde dich sofort feuern." She giggles again at Brunhilda's glare. "Now, off you go to the doggy box." She waves a hand towards the set of double stairs that curve towards each other as they ascend and descend.

Brunhilda rolls her eyes, speaking in a thick Germain accent. "Yes, Mrs. Grüber, I'll clean your precious puppy's shit box." She offers an overly sarcastic grin and then moves to the stairs.

Merrien smiles, nodding once, and turns to the kitchen. "Bet your sweet ass you will." She clicks on the kitchen TV, opening the fridge.

The lady on the news speaks enthusiastically to the camera. "And in other news, the latest attraction to hit the nation is that of Sykes Manor, a haunted house of horror sure to scare the socks off anyone who enters. In the last three years it has amassed hundreds of thousands of dollars from it being open year round for horror and fear-factor fans alike." She laughs, turning to her cohost. "I sure don't like being scared, but I may just have to for this next part." They laugh together as she turns back to the camera. "The mysterious owner is offering to send twelve people inside for a private party where one of them could go home with one hundred thousand dollars if they 'survive the night.'" She shudders. "Oooh, sounds spooky, doesn't it, Tom?" She turns to her cohost.

Tom nods. "It sure does, Janet. It sure does." He chuckles, glancing at her, and taps his papers on their desk. "I may just have to enter myself." He grins, turning back to the camera. "You have a chance to get your golden invitation in the mail, and all you have to do is send in your information through the website www.sykesmanor.com, which is also linked to Facebook, Twitter, Instagram..." He pauses, squinting, and speaks slower. "StumbleUpon, Delicious, and Buzznet." He chuckles, turning to Janet. "Wow, seems I'm behind the times." He shakes his head. "I haven't heard of the last few." He and Janet laugh, both turning to the prompters, and he nods once to the camera. "When we come back, pandemonium at the Brenton Mall." He points to the camera. "Now for the break." The TV switches to an Arby's commercial.

Merrien mulls over the information delivered. "One hundred thousand dollars wouldn't be a bad steal. Maybe once the old stiff is gone, I can mooch off that sad bastard." She grins to herself, leaning her elbows on the large purple marble island, and taps her pink lips with her perfect French tips. "How hard could it be to make it through a cheap haunted house?" Shrugging, she pushes off the island and opens her Fiji water, puts a straw in the bottle, and sips.

———

Back in the smalltime news office:

The blonde sits on the corner of the desk again and buttons her blouse, grinning to herself, and cuts her eyes at Tyler.

Tyler leans back in his seat, swiveling it from side to side with a wide grin of his own. He runs a hand through his sweaty curls, letting out a long sigh, and swings his head towards her.

The blonde giggles. "Good enough inspiration?" She smooths out her hair, twisting it up into a bun again, and stabs the chopsticks through it in an X shape.

Tyler chuckles. "Overdue and underrated with an exceptional cast." He leans forward, resting his laced fingers on the edge of the desk, and smiles up at her.

The blonde smirks, leaning forward, and rests her fingertips under his chin. "Glad I could be of service." She slides from her perch, knocking off a stack of newspapers. "Oh, shit. Sorry!" She bends down to pick them up and stops, staring at the one on top. "Oh! I've heard of this!" She looks up at him, swiping her bangs from her face. "Yea, it's that haunted house thing that's giving away one hundred thousand dollars to whoever can make it for the night." She hands the paper to him.

Tyler opens the page all the way, reading it over. "It's a contest for just twelve people, and I have to give them my address." He folds the paper. "Oh hell no. This is probably some way for a serial killer to get into people's homes and kill them. I've never even heard of this place. And no wonder, it's in bumfuck Mississippi." He slaps the paper on the desk.

The blonde shrugs, cutting her eyes at the paper. "It's been all over the news stations. Supposed to be some overnight sensation." Sighing, she leans her butt against the desk, resting her hands in front of her. "Seems to me it's an easy cash grab." She arches an eyebrow, resting her chin on her shoulder, and glares at him.

Tyler swipes a hand over his face, leaving it over his mouth. "That money would be a good start." He chuckles, letting his hand drop.

The blonde leans towards him, resting her fingers under his

chin. "If you win, come find me." With one last quick kiss, she sexy walks out of the room.

Tyler leans back, putting his hands behind his head, and stares at the picture of Sykes Manor on the front page of his research resource and competitor, the New York Times. "Well, it wouldn't hurt to at least see if I'm drawn." Leaning forward, he snatches the paper, skimming for ways to enter, and moves to the website on his Mac.

CHAPTER TWO
MIAMI, FL, MIAMI-DADE COUNTY COURTHOUSE

Miku stands behind a small table along with a chubby man with a mustard stain on his tie from his over-dressed hot dog lunch. She pulls at the hem of her black blazer, letting her fingers brush along her matching pencil skirt. Walking from behind the table, she addresses the jury with a smile.

The prosecutor and mousy accuser dressed in a nineties dark plaid jumper dress and large clogs stand as well and turn to the jury in irritation.

The judge raises a hand to the jury. "Do you have your final verdict?" Lowering his hand, he rests his fingers along his jaw and cheek and waits.

The foreman stands. A squat man with a military haircut and round wire glasses. He holds a sheet of paper in his shaking hands and refuses to look at anyone or anything but the sheet.

Clearing his throat, the foreman begins to read from the page in a quivering voice. "We, the jury, find Mr. Attleman on the count of sexual assault… not guilty." He pauses as the courtroom erupts into jeers and heckling. "On the count of criminal sexual contact, we find Mr. Attleman… not guilty." He hands the sheet to the bailiff, who hands it to the judge.

More jeers, boos, heckling, and yelling swallow the room. The bailiffs stand ready with their hands on their guns. The judge bangs his gavel to no end, yelling over the crowd. "Order! I will have order in my courtroom! Quiet!" He keeps banging it until silence slinks its way through the room as those with sense quiet down and those without are escorted through the doors, and once silence is found, he addresses the jury. "The jury is thanked for their verdict and excused." He turns to the room, grasping the handle of his gavel, and raises it. "Court is adjourned." Banging the gavel, he hangs his head.

Miku shakes hands with the defendant, who grins from ear to ear as he glares at the crying accuser.

The prosecutor meanders over to Miku. "Well, congratulations on being a world-class cunt... as always." He adjusts his coat over his arm, flexing his grip on his briefcase handle.

Miku grins, standing tall, and grips her briefcase's handle in front of her with both hands. "And as always, you're going straight to the insult without wining and dining me first." She clicks her tongue, tilting her head. "You know I like to be full and drunk before a flaccid fuck so at least I have the numbed-over illusion it was satisfying." With a light giggle, she shrugs, standing straighter and taller. "Why don't you try making sure your case is well put together and believable instead? I did my job... as always." Cocking her head again, she smiles and winks at him.

The prosecutor rolls his eyes, standing as tall as he can, and pushes past her through the little flap gate and out of the room.

Miku smirks to herself, shaking her head a couple times, and then saunters from the room with her head held high.

———

MIAMI, FL, LE PETIT CHAMPIGNON

14

Paulina stands behind a girl stirring a pot of soup. The girl's hand shakes as she raises the tasting spoon to her lips and slurps.

Paulina shrugs (shrugs is correct, means to raise them and lower them quickly like shoulders) her lips. "Well, how do you think it tastes?" She leans forward, looking the dish over, and takes in a deep breath. "Because it smells like a homeless woman's vagina." Glaring at the girl, she raises her eyebrows. "Does it taste like a homeless woman's vagina?" She holds her glare.

The girl sniffles, fighting back tears, and sets the spoon down.

Paulina shakes her head, putting her palms out at her sides. "Well?!" Her voice gets louder, tone rising three octaves.

The girl bursts out crying, and her voice shakes. "It tastes like a homeless woman's vagina." She sobs into her hands.

Paulina huffs, pointing to the door of the kitchen. "Go shit your pants, clean up, and start over." She shakes her pointed finger and bobs her head, making her red curls bounce.

The girl runs from the kitchen, letting out squeals through her sobs.

Paulina huffs, turning to the soup, and brings the spoon to her lips. "Now, is it really that bad?" Slurping up the remaining soup, she shrugs her lips and lays the spoon down. "Needs some salt… and more garlic, but it's not bad." Setting the spoon down, she turns on the TV while waiting for the girl to come back, flipping through the channels.

Channel nine news catches her attention with a picture of Sykes Manor, and she stops.

The brunette lady on the news speaks skeptically to the camera as she reads the prompter. "The most talked about attraction lately is a place called Sykes Manor. Said to be the most exciting haunted house of horror in America. Three years here and it's had hundreds of thousands of dollars made from its year-round open door for those who like to have heart attacks."

She laughs, turning to her cohost. "Would you risk dying for this next part?" They laugh together.

Paulina loses interest, turning back to the soup, and adds a hefty amount of salt, stirring, and lifts the spoon back to her lips. "Eh..." She quirks her lips. "It's better, but still needs garlic." She turns away from the soup and TV, reaching for fresh garlic cloves.

Watching her co-anchor's wide eyes glare back at her, the brunette anchor turns back to the camera. "This unknown owner is offering twelve people a free inside look and a private party. If they stay the whole night, they could win one hundred thousand dollars." She shudders. "Sounds a bit suspicious, don't you think, Gerry?" She turns to her cohost.

Paulina quits chopping, glancing over her shoulder at the TV, letting it hold her attention at the mention of money. "That would be perfect to start expanding." She turns around all the way, listening closer.

Gerry looks down at their desk, shaking his head a few times. "I don't know, Carol, that amount sounds worth it to me." He chuckles, glancing at her, and taps his papers on their desk, letting them flop over his hands. "I sort of want to enter myself." He grins, turning back to the camera. "If you're interested, you can get your golden invitation in the mail. There are several ways to enter your information as well."

Paulina scrambles to find a pen and paper, grabbing a brown paper sack off a counter and a pen from her pocket.

The male anchor continues. "Enter through the website, www.sykesmanor.com, which is linked to Facebook, Twitter, Instagram..." He shifts in his seat, squinting at the prompter. "StumbleUpon, Delicious, and Buzznet." He chuckles, turning to Carol. "Wow, I may have to enter through them all." He shakes his head, laughing with Carol, and he nods once to the camera as they both turn around. "When we come back, we'll let Dr. Garret show you how to lose that stubborn belly fat." He points to the camera. "Now for the break." The TV switches to a movie preview.

Paulina sighs, glancing down at the list of entry options. "I'm going to get my second restaurant." She grins at the page of scribbled writing, and then a figure takes up her right periphery.

The girl stands in the doorway, wringing her apron. "I'm ready to try again." Chewing the corner of her mouth, she looks at Paulina in spurts.

Paulina jerks around, putting the paper in her apron pocket, and tosses a thumb toward the soup. "Well?" She pauses, glaring. "Why're you just standing around? Get to work!" Putting her fists on her hips, she stares at the girl, watching her move around the kitchen.

———

In a three-bedroom, two and a half bath apartment in the nice part of Miami, Miku opens the door, setting her briefcase on the floor to her left, keys on the hook above it, and puts her shoes on the mat to her right behind the door. "Paulina! I'm home!" Closing the door, she set to relocking it and undoes her blazer as she walks farther inside.

Paulina pops her head around the corner from the kitchen, flour smudging her face. "NO! Don't come in here yet! You're early!" She ducks back into the kitchen, and clanking calls out.

Miku giggles, craning her neck in an overdramatic attempt to view past the corner. "What're you making? And yea, I won, again… So we got to go home sooner than we thought." She tosses her blazer over the back of a bar stool and meanders into the living room.

Paulina calls from the kitchen, "It's a surprise—congrats on your win, and I have some small goodish news."

Miku plops onto the white sectional sofa, stretching her legs out over the lounge area. "Oh? What's that?" She unbuttons the top three buttons of her white blouse and lays her head against the back of the couch, closing her eyes.

Paulina giggles a bit. "I entered both of us into this contest for a hundred thousand dollars. All we have to do is stay all night in a haunted house thing in Mississippi. And don't worry, I used your work box like you like." She pops around the corner, untying her blue apron, and smiles at Miku.

Miku lifts her head, arching an eyebrow. "A haunted house? How is that even a challenge?" She smirks, looking Paulina up and down. "You know how cute you look when you're dirty from cooking?" Sliding from her seat, she steps up to her, rubbing off some flour with her thumb.

Paulina smiles. "Do you know how hot you are with your shirt unbuttoned like that?" Licking her lips, she pulls her bottom one between her teeth, leaning down, and plants a soft yet firm and passionate kiss upon Miku's lips.

CHAPTER THREE
LAREDO, TX, TASTE OF LAREDO PIZZA-EATING CONTEST

J eb stands over a thirty-six-inch pizza pan, cramming piece after piece into his mouth as a stadium of people cheers, heckles, and boos.

A time clock counts down above him and four other challengers.

The master of ceremonies throws out a hand to them, putting a mic to his lips. "One minute left on the clock! Quite a few pieces of pizza left on the table, folks! Who will be the next Laredo pizza-eating champion?" He puts out his hands to Jeb and the remaining contestants.

The crowd erupts into cheers. They wave posters, yelling out Jeb's name and blowing fog horns.

Jeb glances around at his competition dipping their pizzas in water, folding them up, and chewing like mad. He turns back to his own pan, dipping his pizza crust a few times in the water cup, and stuffs the slice in his mouth.

The clock behind them gets to ten seconds left.

The crowd counts down with it.

Ten.

Nine.

Eight.

Seven.

Six.

Five.

Four.

Three.

Two.

One!

Pushing the last bite of crust past his teeth, Jeb chews and chews, forcing the bolus down his gullet with a nice swig of water to help it slide down easier.

The clock stops, letting out a loud alert.

Standing tall, Jeb puts his hands over his stomach. Puffing out his cheeks, he fights back vomit. Swallowing it back, he opens his mouth, sticking out his tongue.

The crowd goes wild.

The judge walks up to him, putting his right arm in the air.

Jeb raises his free arm, too, pumping his fists above his head.

The other contestants growl, shaking their heads, and throw the remainder of their pizza back on the pan. One guy runs to the back of the stage and pukes over the stage railings into the grass. Another starts crying, putting his hands over his face.

A very upset-looking woman approaches him, putting her arms over the backs of his shoulders. "It's alright, Johnny, we'll make up the money some other way." She pats him as they walk off stage.

The master of ceremonies hands Jeb a trophy with one hundred thousand dollars in the cup, shaking his hand, and they turn forward for flashing pictures.

Jeb glances over his shoulder, catching the crying man and the woman, having overheard what she said, and leaves the master standing in front of the camera.

As he approaches the couple, the woman looks up, rubbing the man's shoulders. "Can I help you?" She glances at the man sitting with his face in his hands.

Jeb hands her the stack of cash. "I, uh, I don't need it." Shrugging, he takes a step back.

The woman looks at the money in her hands, speechless, and nudges the man with her elbow. "Johnny. Johnny! Look!" With wide eyes and huge smile, she holds up the cash to him.

Johnny refrains from his moping, leaning up, and stops short, cutting his eyes at Jeb. "What's this? Some kinda charity?" He shoots from his seat, pointing at Jeb. "You think I got my hand out?" His face turns redder than before, and he holds his finger out, poking Jeb's beefy chest.

Jeb puts up his hands, tilting his head down, and glances at the ground. "Look, buddy, Johnny is it? I just happened to hear what your woman said, and I thought I'd help. I don't need the money more so than I wanted the title." He shrugs, keeping his hands up, and flexes his overly large arms.

Johnny stands tall, crossing his arms, and then wipes his mouth a few time, glancing over his shoulder at the woman and the cash. "Well, thank you. We defaulted on a loan and needed the money to pay it off and some of the house note." Shrugging, he shakes his head, putting out a hand.

Jeb glances from the hand to Johnny's eyes and grips it. "No problem. We all fall on hard times." Nodding to him and her, he turns away.

A scrawny man about a foot shorter than Jeb steps up to him in a Def Leppard T-shirt, cargo khaki shorts, and black low-top Converse, and he slaps a hand on the middle of Jeb's back. "Hey, man, I know they were all like, 'We need money,' but so do you. Or did you forget?" Cutting his eyes up, he arches an eyebrow at Jeb.

Jeb rolls his eyes, shaking his head a bit. "It'll be ok, Kik, I can win the next competition and get the money back. Willard will understand." He turns to Kik, nodding a few times.

Kik rolls his eyes, face-palming himself, and huffs. "C'mon, J, you know better than I do that Willard doesn't do second chances." He points behind them. "That was our meal ticket out from under him. He's not a nice dude." He puts both hands out at his legs. "And I, for one, like having the use of my legs." Arching his eyebrow again, he cuts his eyes up, putting out his hands.

Jeb chuckles deep in his massive chest, scratching it, and looks ahead of them as they walk. "I'll make it back, I promise." He stops walking, hitting the side of his fist against his chest, and lets out a huge and loud burp that seems to never end. "Whoo! I feel loads better." Laughing, he turns to Kik.

Kik just glares at him. "Dude, drink some mouthwash." He fans a hand in front of his face. "That's rank." Grimacing, he leans back, still fanning. "And how do you plan on winning the money back, huh? The next contest is in a month. You have like three weeks. He won't wait much longer." Shrugging, he puts out both hands, holding them there.

Jeb shrugs too, shaking his head, and looks off to the other side of the park, stopping short, and points. "There." He wags his pointed finger at a poster on a wire pole, and they walk up to it.

Kik runs his finger under the words, stopping at 'one hundred thousand dollars.' "Jeb." He hits Jeb's chest with the back of his hand, cocking his head up. "I do believe you've done something right... for once." Chuckling, he pulls out his phone, taking a picture of the announcement poster for Sykes Manor's one-night party prize.

Jeb nudges him with a beefy elbow, pointing to the super tiny words at bottom of the poster. "Says the cutoff for entries is tomorrow. And the party is in two weeks. The winners will receive their invitations next week." Smirking, he turns to Kik. "If we blow up the entries, we have better odds of getting chosen, aaand we can pay Willard back ahead of time." Holding his smirk, he winks.

Kik puts his phone in his pocket, shoving his hands into his pockets right after, and nods to his left. "You got any room left?

He tosses his head towards the sub shop across the way from their spot, and pats his growling stomach with a grin.

Jeb puts a meaty fist to Kik's shoulder, giving it a nudge. "Yea, man, I'm actually in the mood for something sweet." He rolls his tongue along his mouth, smacking a few times. "Hope they got cookies." Licking his lips, he scratches his large, broad chest, stretching a bit.

Kik rubs his shoulder, shaking his head with a smirk and chuckle, and then leads the way.

———

FINALE LIGURE, ITALY, VOGUE PHOTO SHOOT

Cameras click and flash back to back.

Three women, who look as if they haven't had a period since they were fifteen, pose around a tall and lean Blake, whose long hair billows and whips around his head and shoulders. Their dark clothes and dramatic hair and makeup press against a bright blue sky overlooking a beach.

Blake holds the edges of a popped black blazer collar as he stares off at nothing in particular. He lets the women lean on him, hug on him, and slide their arms all over him for the next hour as they change positions from standing to sitting to lounging. By the end of the hour, during wardrobe and makeup changes, he relaxes in his makeup chair while the artist moves around him.

A small girl with a bright blonde messy bun dressed in jeans and a blues festival T-shirt moves every which way, putting on a thin layer of foundation while speaking into her Bluetooth. "Yea, Mama, I read about the party on my phone. I'm going to enter either way." She laughs, crossing her fingers. "Fingers crossed I'm back in the states by then." She pauses, dabbing some pale pink blush onto Blake's cheeks. "Oh, I know. I hope to buy a house with it. One hundred thousand dollars is big money to us poor folks." Laughing, she turns around to the mirror, setting down the palette. "Yea, Mama, okay. Love you too. Bye." Taking out the Bluetooth, she turns back to Blake. "Sorry about that." She offers a squinting grin. "My mom can be a bit long-winded sometimes." Rolling her eyes, she flips and flops her hand in the air.

Blake shifts in the cloth seat. "No problem." He pauses, lifting a finger from the narrow wooden chair arm. "What exactly were you two taking about?" He closes his eyes upon her approach.

The artist giggles. "She had seen on the news about the haunted house, Sykes Manor, holding a random-pick contest dinner party for twelve folks to win one hundred thousand dollars if they can last all night." She dabs some blue eyeshadow on his lids. "I was telling her I'm gonna enter tonight." She laughs through her nose, adding some gel to his eyebrows to keep them against the grain. "I doubt I'll be picked, but I'll never know unless I enter." Finishing, she brushes her hands against each other and sighs.

Blake sighs with a smirk, tossing his chin at her. "You unfortunately don't get picked, you wanna go out to dinner with me?" He sits tall, holding her gaze.

The artists lets a hard, loud laugh escape, immediately covering her mouth, and talks through her fingers. "Maybe ask me again when you don't look like an Asian clown." Giggling, she walks off, no longer impeding the mirror.

Blake stares at the makeup job ordered by the modeling company and snarls, growling to himself. Damn. He mulls over the idea of winning that money just for a good vacation. Maybe back in Colorado. Yea. That would be nice, not going home, per se, but getting to live in the nicest lodge and skiing from dawn to dusk. Moving to his duffel sitting near the portable vanity, he pulls out his phone and looks up how to enter.

CHAPTER FOUR
BREAUX BRIDGE, LOUISIANA, IN THE
SECRET BACK ROOM OF BACK WOODS BAR

An older, less gangly and leaner Houston sits in a beat up old computer chair, slick and shiny green fabric cracking at the seams.

Cigar and cigarette smoke permeates the room, clinging to the humidity in the hot air.

Five other gentlemen sit around the table with him, each one puffing one of the two types of smoke sticks.

A tan blonde woman, probably in her mid-thirties but looking fifty, serves the table a round of beers.

Hugh thumbs over the cards in his hand, glancing at the ones left on the table, and huffs. "I call. All in." Picking up all of his small stack of chips, he tosses them to the pot in the middle.

The man next to him calls.

The man next to him checks.

And the dealer at the end leans back, speaking in a thick Cajun accent. "Alright now, all bets are done." He knocks a few times on the table, eyeing Hugh.

Hugh scratches the back of his thin, disheveled and nappy curls, arching an eyebrow at his cards, and lets that hand swipe over his mouth, scratching his thin goatee.

The other men cut their eyes at him, eyeing their cards, and puff on their smoke sticks.

The first man flips his two cards over, speaking in a thick Cajun as well. "Two pair, fours and queens." Smacking on the end of his cigar, he grumbles under his breath, "Should've folded." Shifting in his seat, he mumbles cuss words in French.

The next man flips his cards, speaking in a Texas drawl. "Three queens and two sixes." He smirks, patting the first man's shoulder.

The first man snatches his shoulder away, swatting at the guy, and mumbles more French.

Hugh's turn, and he swallows against a dry mouth. "Well, y'all." He glances around the table. "Y'all've bested me once again." He gives them a halfhearted chuckle, swallowing against sand paper, and flips over his cards. "I've got nothing." He gives them another halfhearted chuckle. "What can I say? Y'all called my bluff." Heat radiates from below his sweat-soaked shirt, hitting his chin and cheeks.

The men growl, dealer leaning forward across the table at him. "You sayin' you're out of money?" Leaning back, he crosses his arms.

Hugh glances around the room full of burly men with guns and swallows harder against his ever drying mouth. "If you could just lend me a little more, I'm sure I can win it back. I'm just going through a gambler's drought is all." He flops his hands to either side of him, then puts them up at the glaring men. "C'mon guys, what about good old Southern hospitality? Huh?" He pauses, glancing around with an awkward grin plastered across his face.

The next thing he knows, one of the burly men is tossing him out the back door, across the narrow alley, and into the brick wall of the next building.

Coughing, Hugh gets to his forearms and knees slow.

The guy who threw him yells in deep and thick Cajun, "Get us the money, or you won't be able to walk." Turning away, he slams the door shut behind him.

Hugh groans out his words, talking to the guy, but really talking to himself. "How will I get the money if I can't walk to make it?" Coughing, he groans again, putting a hand to his stomach, and looks up.

A hot pink page of laminated paper flaps against a power pole a few yards down the alley, making a loud fwacking sound over and over.

Getting to his feet, Hugh walks down the alley in the direction of the pole, intent on turning away from it and going to his right, but the image and giant text blaring "one hundred thousand dollars" on the flyer catches his eye.

In the middle of the paper, in fading black ink, is a picture of Sykes Manor. The info is listed around the pic and at the bottom.

Pulling out his phone, the screen now busted at a corner, he enters every possible way.

SANTA FE, NEW MEXICO

Sitting in the middle of her living room in a pure white leather gaming chair, Brenda clicks away on her Xbox controller, speaking into her headset. "Okay, guys, you have got to get it together. We canNOT lose this tdm. I have a lot of money riding on it." Toggling her joy stick, she holds down the trigger button, shooting one of the opponents dead.

Rapid firing and explosions come from the massive speakers on either side of her multi-monitor gaming station.

A male voice comes from the speaker on her headset. "Don't lose full, Bubbles, we're valid, girl."

Brenda watches a grenade hit one of her partners. "Damn it, Reggie! I told you to watch your minimap and stay aware! Stop being such a fucking burger!" She grip her controller tighter, clicking and toggling away, hitting every target.

A distressed male voice comes over her headset. "I'm not a

burger, Bubbles, you fuckin' bitch! Stop yellin' at me! I made one mistake!"

Bubbles lets out a shrill, borderline hysterical laugh. "Yea, a mistake that put us over the death toll and cost us the fucking match! Ugh!" In her rage, she throws her controller across the room, hitting the back of her chair.

Multiple voices, female and male, come over the headset, speaking all at once.

"Don't be like that, Bubbles."

"C'mon, girl, it's one match."

"You can't win every time."

"How much money did you bet on us?"

The last question makes her stop pacing the room and push her short bleach-blonde hair away from her face with a huff. "Fifty thousand." She huffs, letting her hand slide over her face, and it stops at her mouth.

The voices begin again.

"Damn, B. Why so much?"

"What were you thinking? We don't even get paid that much to play."

"Where'd you get the money, and why didn't you tell us about it?"

Brenda whimpers into her hand a bit before huffing again. "I have been saving up my winnings…" She turns in a quick circle to face the screen showing XP and the few unlocked items, and her voice shakes. "And then one night, someone on the other team IM'ed me, betting that they could beat us with extremely specific guidelines surrounding their hypothesis…" Her eyes widen as they fall to the floor, and she shakes her head as if they can see her. "And clearly they were wrong, but fucking Reggie had to swoop down and get hit by a motherfucking rogue grenade to tip us over the edge." She points her whole hand out in front of her as if they can see it and grits her teeth.

Reggie's voice comes back over the headset a smooth and deep tone. "It. Wasn't. My. Fault. That grenade came out of

DEATH INVITES IN GOLD

nowhere, and the game just glitched to give them the win. I was in the midst of moving away. I wasn't even near it. We got joked."

An ache builds in the pit of Brenda's stomach, and she sighs, pinching the bridge of her nose as she closes her eyes. "If that's true, Reggie, then I owe you an apology." Letting go of the bridge of her nose, she returns to her screen, opening the dialogue box, displaying a root screen. "I'm going to look into the code to see if it was a true glitch." She rolls out her wireless keyboard, tapping away on the silicone covered keys.

Her headset goes quiet.

Brenda falls back into the chair, letting it swivel, and huffs. "It was a true glitch." Slapping her hand against her forehead, she mumbles out her words. "Sorry, Reggie." Cutting her eyes to her left, she growls to herself.

Reggie's voice comes over her headset a bit lighter-hearted than before. "Thanks, Bubs." He sniggers, then one of the screens shows him signing off.

Brenda sighs again, swiveling herself with her toe. "I'll catch you guys later, I gotta figure out how to get my money back." Before any of them can respond, she turns off her headset, tapping a few keys, and turns off all the screens except the main one.

A text box pops up in the bottom right corner of the screen advertising a contest.

Intrigued, Brenda clicks on it. "Probably spam, but it's worth a peek." Shrugging, she skims over the larger text box that takes up half her screen.

A flashing light display surrounds a collage of pictures featuring guts, blood, and gore. The middle picture is that of Sykes Manor in black and white for ominous effect.

Brenda squints at the screen, breathing out her words. "What the fuck is this?" Turning on the screens again, she switches her headset on, peeking at the online list.

Dedric is still on.

Good.

Brenda adjusts the mic in front of her mouth. "Hey, D." She waits.

Dedric sighs into his mic. "Yea, girl?"

Brenda smiles to herself, cheeks getting a bit warm. "I just got this pop-up for a haunted house contest; the winnings are a hundred K if you last the night." She sniggers. "You in? All we gotta do is enter with our name and address." Leaning back, she swivels. "Or do you think it's spam? 'Cause I haven't heard of Sykes Manor." She rests her elbow on her chair arm, plopping her chin in her hand, and waits for him to respond.

A light sniggering comes across the headset. "B, I signed up for that weeks ago. Today's the final entry day. That place is supposed to be the shit of haunted houses, like total top-notch scare-you-shitless type of horror. Go for it, girl!"

Brenda bites her bottom lip, and then realization hits, and she furrows her eyebrows. "You've known about this for weeks, and you're just now telling me? I told you minutes after finding out about it." She sits straight, eyeing the void between her and her keyboard.

Dedric chuckles. "Sorry, B, didn't know at the time it would be such a big deal. I wasn't even sure it was your scene." He gives her that same charming chuckle.

Brenda rolls her eyes to herself, shaking her head, and grins. "It's fine, but next time, remember it's totally my scene." She smirks to herself, letting out a light giggle, and cuts off the screens again.

Scrolling down the ad, she gets to the entry point, putting in her info, and then cuts off the last screen, going into the kitchen for a turkey sandwich.

CHARLOTTE, NORTH CAROLINA, RIVER JAM RUN: RACE EDITION
TRIATHLON

Dorine crosses the finish line of her final race seconds after her main opponent and slows, catching her breath. "As always, Marci, good run." Bringing a hand down from her head, she extends it, taking a deep breath.

Marci grins, taking her hand, and shakes, catching her own breath. "Same to you." Gulping air, she returns her hand to the top of her head, letting her breath out slow.

Breaths normalizing, they meander over to the water station, picking up the small red paper cups, and drink their fill without over drinking or getting brain freeze from its cold. On the other side of the table next to them are the water station attendants chatting away.

Dorine leans toward them. "What was that you said about a contest?" She eyes the bleach blonde, giving her a grimace for eavesdropping.

The bleach blonde puts her hands on her hips. "There's this haunted house in Mississippi holding a contest to see who can stay the entire night for a hundred thousand dollars." Her eyebrow twitches, and she snarls.

Dorine cuts her eyes at Marci and smirks. "Oh, that sounds pretty cool." She returns her gaze to the bleach blonde, standing taller. "I've never heard of it, though." Smiling dramatically, she bats her eyelashes a few times.

The bleach blonde rolls her eyes.

The dirty blonde to her left lets out a hard laugh, addressing Dorine. "You're kidding, right?" She eyes Dorine, arching an eyebrow.

Dorine sniggers to Marci, shaking her head. "We've been training for the Olympics. We've barely had time to pee, let alone do anything fun." She sniggers again, nudging Marci with her elbow.

The dirty blonde eyes the two of them, mouth hanging open a bit. "It's like the hottest attraction of horror in the US right now. How have you not seen, like, a commercial or heard about it through, like, a podcast, or even on the news before now?" She lets out a few forced breathy laughs, never taking her eyes off them.

Dorine raises her eyebrows, eyes widening for a second, and she giggles, cutting her eyes at Marci. "So, how do I enter into this super-hot contest?" Waving fanned fingers a few times, she crosses her arms over her running tank, and her racing number crinkles.

Both girls shake their heads, but the bleach blonde answers. "Oh, no… you two can figure that out on your own. I think we've helped out enough." Giving them an overly scrunched smirk, she crosses her arms, staring them both down.

Dorine and Marci giggle, speaking in unison. "Alright…" Giggling more, they move off and away from the girls and crowd.

Sitting on a bench, Dorine turns to Marci. "Wanna enter together? We can split the winnings." Squinting, she looks up at her, letting the upturned corner of her mouth part her lips.

Marci sighs, searching the ground at her feet. "I donno, D. Like you said, we barely have enough time to pee, let alone have fun. Besides, we don't have much training time left, and this is so on the spot. When do they even draw, and what night is it for?" She chews the corner of her mouth.

Dorine leans forward in her seat, propping her elbows on her knees. "Well, let's look it up." She pulls out her phone, opening her Google app, and types in the search bar. "Says here that today is the last day to enter, the drawing is tonight, they announce the winners next week, and the party is the week after." She returns her squinting gaze to Marci. "So, wanna split the winnings?" She smirks.

Marci chews the corner of her mouth again. "Well, this leaves one question, is the money per winner or one lump sum?" She grins.

Dorine laughs, scrolling through the ways to enter. "That's my girl." Scooting over for Marci to sit, they fill in the entry forms with their info.

CHAPTER FIVE
REDONDO BEACH, CALIFORNIA, RBPD
INTERROGATION ROOM

Nathan sits in the uncomfortable metal chair with minimal cushioning, arms crossed over the table's edge, and his head lies on his wrists. His bleach-blonde dreads hang about his shoulders, neck, and biceps.

The door screeches opens.

Nathan lifts his head, bloodshot and dark-circled eyes narrowing at the cop across the table. "So, Officer Corey, was my info good?" Huffing, he wipes over his sunken and thin face with both hands, sitting up and leaning back in the chair.

Corey plops a Smashburger to-go bag on the table. The scent of mushroom, swiss, onions, and fries fills the room.

Nathan licks his lips, leaning forward, and reaches for the bag.

Corey slides it just out of reach. "Not so fast, Nathan. Your info was good. We got what we needed, but you gotta get clean, man." He pauses, huffing, and lowers his voice. "For both our sakes." Wiping his mouth, he pushes the bag toward Nathan.

Nathan snatches the bag. Pulling it up to his face, he peers inside. Leaning back, he reaches in, paper crinkling, and pulls out a huge burger. After that a carboard container of fries. Eyeing Corey, he unwraps the burger, shoving it in his mouth.

Corey leans back with a sigh, wiping his mouth again, and watches Nathan gorge himself.

Nathan swallows, taking a sip from his to-go cup, and crams more into his mouth, speaking through the food. "I know, pig. I know." He holds up the burger with a chipmunk grin. "Thanks for the food." Letting some squish from his lips, he resumes an open-mouth chew.

Corey grimaces, rolling his eyes, and forces himself to ignore the echoing smacks. "Yea, sure." Swallowing against the vomit in his throat, he waits the eternity for Nathan to finish eating.

Once done, Nathan lets out a loud burp, shoving the last three fries into his mouth with a smile. "So, take me home?" He sucks the last of his drink, making it do that slurping noise.

Huffing, Corey nods, rising from his seat with a slight grunt. "Yea." He sighs, holding the door handle. "C'mon." He opens the door, glaring at the top of the frame as he waits.

Nathan drags, grabbing his trash, and throws it in the garbage next to the door in the hallway.

The two of them walk through the small police station out to the parking lot, and Nathan gets in the back of Corey's cruiser.

Ten minutes later, Corey stops at an apartment building and gets out, opening the back driver-side door. "Go inside, get cleaned up. I'll be off work in a few hours." He huffs, meeting Nathan's smirk, and glares off at nothing in particular. "Damn, I'm glad I already got your part of the rent when your check came." He rolls his tongue along his mouth, cutting his eyes at Nathan. "Get out." He steps aside, holding the door.

Nathan sniggers, scooting across the plastic bucket seats, and laughs as he gets out. "Yea, I'll be squeaky clean when you get home." Chuckling, he shakes his head, pulling the keys from his pocket, and limps his way inside.

Shaking his head, Corey slams the car door shut, watching him go inside the apartment, and then returns to work.

Another hour and a half later, Corey sits at his desk, scrolling through Facebook while nibbling on the leftover half of a

Subway sandwich. Taking a bite, he scrolls up to an ad for Sykes Manor. It details the contest and entry paths as well as pictures of the attraction. He taps on the link, and it takes him to a separate Safari page to enter.

Hesitating a bit, Corey mumbles to himself, "What the hell." Tapping the address box, he puts in his post office box address.

When done, Corey pauses as an idea crosses his mind. Taking the plunge, he enters Nathan with their apartment address. Sitting back, he curves his fingers over his lips, staring at the confirmation of entry taking up the screen. Closing the window, he puts his phone down and gets on with the rest of his paperwork, letting it fall from his mind.

———

Later that evening, the clock shows the end of shift, and Corey grabs his jacket and keys, getting in his cruiser. After pulling up to the apartment building, he loosens his tie, fiddling with his keys until he finds the right one, and unlocks the door.

Pulling the key from the lock, Corey glances around the entrance to their dark, modest two-room one-bath apartment. "Hey, Nate! I'm home! Hope you haven't eaten the rest of my Cocoa Pebbles." Chuckling, he arches an eyebrow at the quiet darkness. "Hey! Why're all the lights off? We talked about leaving this one on for me to walk inside with." Groaning, he closes the door with a soft click, waiting and listening for a reply.

Nothing.

That's strange. He always lets out some sort of sarcastic answer. A sudden panic sets in, and Corey moves toward Nathan's room in the back of the apartment.

The door is cracked enough of a sliver that the catch touches metal to metal.

A light flashes from inside, and a soft conversation leaks through.

Corey puts his hand to the door, hesitating against the truth he might find. Swallowing hard, he pushes the door, cracking it a bit more. It screeches on its hinges, and his heart drops at the sight it reveals.

There, sprawled over the bed, is Nathan. Skinny bungee cord lying loose under his arm. Needle on the floor below his bleached-blonde hanging hair. Lifelessness in his glazed over eyes. Mouth hanging open in a slight smile as a line of foaming vomit trails up his cheek. It still drips to the floor.

Coming to his senses, Corey rushes into the room, pressing two fingers in the crook at the base of Nathan's jaw.

Nothing.

Corey leans over, putting an ear to Nathan's lukewarm chest. No rise or fall. No sound whatsoever.

Wiping his mouth with the hand he didn't use to check Nathan's pulse, he huffs, mulling over his options. The best possible course is to rub down most things he would touch every day, like the doorknobs, the counters, the dishes, and the cabinets, and then call in as a concerned citizen of the building. Lucky for him, Mr. Narz across the hall calls about Nate all the time when he's at work. He also has no idea Corey lives there.

After everything has been wiped down, he opens and closes the front door with a rag, heads downstairs, and calls in with his best old man voice.

Minutes later, the call comes over the comms, and Corey intercepts, waiting a few minutes before walking back inside. Once inside, he uses the comm to call in the code for a junkie death.

The unis and forensics come out, take photos and collect evidence from the room but go nowhere else in the apartment. Case open and shut.

Simple.

Corey, on the other hand, fights to keep his cool. He actually liked Nate, and the sniggering condolences of his fellow officers add to his cover-up guilt.

CHAPTER SIX
CHARLOTTE, NORTH CAROLINA

Dorine walks into her studio apartment, plopping the mail on the counter, and puts her keys in the bowl by the door. Kicking off her shoes, she goes into the kitchen and makes herself a glass of water. While chugging her water, a flash catches her eye. Furrowing her eyebrows, she moves towards the stack of mail, spreading it all out. In the middle of the stack is a thin, shining golden envelope with her address in scrolling script but no return address. Opening it, she pulls out a single sheet of heavy cardstock flaked with gold and embossed with black. In big bold script are the words:

Congratulations Lucky Winner of this Golden Invitation!

- *Wear a costume of your choice. One that can't possibly show any part of your true identity.*
- *Create a persona around that costume. A fool-proof one that no one could guess you if they know you.*
- *Stick to the persona, revealing nothing about your true self, or else you forfeit your rights to the game, and so will be sent home.*

- *No substitutions. If you don't come with valid identification to prove yourself at the door, you forfeit.*
- *You must have the invitation with you, or you forfeit.*

Upon receiving your invitation, do not tell the press, or anyone else.

Enclosed are specific details for your evening's transportation.

Dorine shrugs her lips, flipping the card over to a blank and dented gold back. Flipping it upright, she grins. Grabbing her phone, she texts Marci her good news and then with her help sets to figuring out the best costume.

———

Santa Fe, New Mexico

Brenda sits in front of her screens, clicking away on her controller, and shoots her way through Halo.

A clinking comes from across the room, hitting her one ear without the headset speaker against it.

Not wanting to take her eyes off the game, she ignores it until a bunch of envelopes start plopping onto the floor at the base of her front door. Rolling her eyes, Brenda pauses her game, slamming her headset into her seat, and stomps to the scattered stack of mail. Cycling through the oddly large stack, a golden envelope catches her eye. Eyes widening, her heart races as she rips it open, pulls out the slip of cardstock, and reads over the words and instructions. Jumping in place, she jerks still, staring into the void between her and the rest of the room, and then abandons her game for Google's costume suggestions.

———

BREAUX BRIDGE, LOUISIANA

Hugh rolls off the couch to the stained shag carpet below. The beer bottles clank into each other as he hits them, doing his best to get up.

Rubbing the butt of his palm over his eyes, he mumbles to himself, "Bet if I hadn't lost the last tournament I'd be sippin' Mai Tais in Mexico right now instead of stale beer in this dump." He laughs, letting it turn into a sad giggle as he wipes the same hand over his face. "Ugh, Hugh, what have you let happen to yourself?" Huffing, he forces himself to stand, shuffling across the carpet, and puts on some pants.

After a few minutes of waking up, Hugh makes his way down the stairs to his mailbox. Turning the key, he opens it to one single delivery.

A golden envelope.

Heart racing, he glances around him before pulling the cardstock from it and reads it over, snarling, and groans. "Do I really have to wear a costume?" Huffing, he nods. "It's a hundred thousand dollars, Hugh, you can dress up for one night. Maybe there'll be a hot chick there too." Smirking to himself, he taps the letter against his hand and races upstairs to get dressed.

If he's going to dress up, he needs to find a good costume, and the only place with free computers is the library.

LAREDO, TEXAS

Jeb chows down on a massive burger, bits of it falling onto his plate.

Kik comes through the room, slapping his hand down on the table next to Jeb, and sports a huge smile.

Jeb stops eating mid-chew and arches an eyebrow.

Kik removes his hand, revealing the invitation. "You did it, man! You made it!" Still smiling, he slaps the back of his hand against Jeb's shoulder.

Jeb sets down his burger, picking up the letter, and reads it over with a grimace. "It says I have to dress up and make this fake identity." Shaking his head, he hands it back. "That wasn't in the first description, and I don't do costumes." Shaking his head again, he pick up his burger, taking a huge bite.

Kik rolls his eyes, setting the invite back on the table. "Dude, just think of the money. You can put up with that bullshit for one night." He holds up a finger, leaning down closer to him, and shakes the finger.

Jeb holds eye contact with him for several unwavering seconds and then huffs, rolling his eyes. "Fine!" He swallows. "But make it good; if I'ma do this shit, it can't be half-assed." He shrugs Kik away. "Now let me finish my lunch." Leaning away, he chews with his mouth open until Kik leaves still smiling.

MIAMI, FLORIDA

Walking into work, Miku stops at her mailbox on the first floor. Setting down her briefcase, she unlocks the little door, pulling out the thick stack.

There, amongst the narrow white, is the wide and golden envelope.

Miku glances around her, chewing her bottom lip, and slips the letter out. Her eyes widen as she reads it over. Glancing around one more time, she opens her briefcase and slips it inside.

Later that evening, once home, Paulina greets Miku at the door with a huge smile plastered across her face. "You will never guess what I got in the mail today!" She holds her hands behind her, swaying with excitement.

Miku smirks. "If it's anything like what I got at work, then I might know exactly what you got." She opens her briefcase. "Show on three." She watches Paulina nod. "One, two, three."

She rips the letter from the case, letting the heavy leather drop to the floor.

Both women hold up identical letters.

Paulina lets out a squeal, then just as quick, composes herself.

Miku smirks, shoes clacking as she steps up to her, and she pecks Paulina's lips. "Looks like we're going to need costumes and personas." Arching an eyebrow, she gives her another peck.

———

NEWPORT, RHODE ISLAND

Merrien steps away on her oversized and over-electronic treadmill, watching the giant screen it's Bluetoothing to across the room. The mountainside view has her running down a path as the cool down for her workout.

The doorbell chimes.

Merrien takes in a deep breath, yelling out, "Brunhilda! Get the door, would you?" She waits for an answer.

Nothing.

Growling to herself, Merrien yells louder, "Brunhilda!" Growling at the lack of answer, she cuts off the machine, grabbing a towel, and heads to the front door in her skin-tight yoga pants and tank.

At the door, a mail carrier waits, package and envelopes in hand.

Merrien opens the door a crack, arching an eyebrow at the man, then realizes how cute he is and opens the door all the way. "Can I help you?" She gives him her best smile, looking his toned and taut physique over unashamedly.

The mail carrier clears his throat, giving her a quick glance over. "I have a package for you to sign for." He hands her the brick of an electronic signing pad with a quick grin.

The entire time she signs, Merrien never breaks eye contact or drops her smile. "Thank you." Licking her lips, she lets out a humming sigh.

The mail carrier chuckles, taking the brick back, and exchanges it for her mail. "You have a nice day, ma'am." Nodding once, he turns around to his truck.

Merrien watches his tight ass as he gets farther away. "You, too!" Jerking herself from the doorway, she kicks it closed behind her and flips through the mail.

On the fourth grab and tuck, the golden envelope stops her dead in her tracks.

Merrien breaks it open, pulling the letter from it, and reads it over. Eyes widening, a mischievous grin spreads across her face.

———

NEW YORK CITY, NEW YORK

Tyler sits at his dining table-slash-workspace and bangs his head against the wood with his fingers laced over his neck. "I need a distraction." Getting up, he meanders through the kitchen, then the living room, and then decides to go downstairs.

While down in the lobby of the apartment building, the passersby draw Tyler's attention to the mailboxes across the way. Wouldn't hurt to just check. There's no way he won, though. Unlocking his mailbox, he swings the little door open, stopping dead.

Inside sits a shining golden envelope.

Tyler shakes his head, breathing out his words. "There's no way." Reaching inside, he pulls out the envelope, peeling it open, and slips the letter free. "This can't be happening." His heart pounds in his ears, and his mouth goes dry as he lets out a shrill giggle to himself. "Whaaat?" Reading it over, he wipes his mouth, rolling his eyes. "Guess I need to get a costume, but what could it be?" Huffing, he tucks the letter under his shirt, racing upstairs, and looks up how to do Halloween makeup for dummies.

———

Blake kicks the door open to his apartment, having come home from Italy. Dropping his luggage near the door, he slips, grabbing hold of the frame.

Envelopes slide out from under his foot across the tile.

Rolling his eyes, Blake grumbles under his breath, "Damn mailmen, can't they use my box like normal carriers?" Grumbling, he scoops up the mail, stopping on one in particular.

The golden envelope gleams in the yellow light of his walkway.

Blake brings the envelope to his face, looking it over, but no return address. Then, he slices it open with a letter opener and pulls the cardstock from its confines.

Reading it over, Blake sniggers. "This will be a piece of cake. Personas are my specialty." Sniggering more, he lays the letter down, heading to his closet.

———

REDONDO BEACH, CALIFORNIA

Corey moves through the apartment in silence. The memory of Nathan dead on his bed haunts him. He hasn't been sleeping well. On his way out for work, he stops at the mailbox just in case someone hasn't gotten the news of Nathan's death. Opening the door, he stares at the one piece of mail. Pulling the envelope with Nathan's name on it from the box, he flips it over, peeling the flap free, and pulls out the letter. Reading it over, he chews

RACHEL BROSS

his bottom lip, fighting off the pain and guilt. Pausing for a moment, he taps the letter and envelope against his hand.

Nate would tell him to go. He would say this is a great opportunity for him.

If Nate were still here, Corey would go just to get the money to help him get clean for good, but that pipe dream has sailed. Now the money would be a cleaner, fresher start somewhere else. Maybe somewhere in a quieter, smaller town.

Corey slips the letter in his uniform jacket, getting in his cruiser, and stops at his own P.O. box for good measure. Opening it up, he finds nothing more than bills and ads. His stomach churns, but he swallows back the guilt, taking the letter, and sets to plan a fool-proof costume as it says to.

CHAPTER SEVEN
THE MIDDLE OF NOWHERE, MISSISSIPPI

A line of black limos makes its way toward what looks to be a rather large house with barbed-wire fencing, a gravel drive, and a lot of grassy pastures. Each limo stops in a single file line along the stairs leading up to the concrete front porch of a large, mostly brick, three-story white plantation-looking house. Multiple arches stand in front of giant windows and a massive black double front door.

Lights flash from within.

The two upper balconies' matching arches guard more windows.

More flashes.

A scream rings out from inside.

Each driver exits their limo, standing at the door of their fare one at a time.

From the first limo juts a metallic hot-pink stiletto and tanned leg. The heel digs into the gravel, making it crunch. Slipping out the back seat, her matching mini skirt glints in waves over her curves as the tight fabric clings a quarter way down her hips. Standing tall, she pulls up on her white tube top, bouncing her size-D breasts behind the large pink Barbie moniker, and giggles as she marvels over the house.

The driver closes her door with a loud click.

Jumping a bit, Barbie puts shaking fingers to her overly teased blonde hair, flitting a hot-pink grin at him. "Sorry, I don't do scary much." Letting out a breathy laugh, she turns towards the house and mumbles, "Couldn't have picked a more hillbilly fuck-me house?" Tugging her hot-pink biker jacket down her shoulders, her every step shakes and wobbles as she crunches her way towards the porch.

From the second limo emerges a black dress shoe that presses down into the gravel, moving back and forth as the rest of him follows. Standing tall, he adjusts his bowtie, straightening his tuxedo lapel, and looks around.

Barbie lets out a yip, grinning his way. "Looking sexy, Mr. Skeleton Man." She eyes him up and down, licking the edge of her upper lip.

Mr. Skeleton Man smirks under his thick black and white makeup and arches an eyebrow her way. "Looking rather delectable yourself there, Barbie." Leaning over a bit, his eyes trail from her toned legs, taut ass, exposed, tan, and toned stomach and breasts, to her bare tanned shoulders.

Barbie bites her tongue, letting out a quick giggle, and then eyes the next limo, drawing his attention there as well.

From the third limo stretches a deep green kitten heel attached to a bright green-covered leg leading up towards a leafy bodysuit. The suit curves and holds tight to a rather curvy bodice. Red hair drapes over pale shoulders, mingling with the vines surrounding slender arms to green nails. A mask of vines surround orange- and pink-shadowed eyes and leads into her hair.

Mr. Skeleton Man lets out a whistle. "Damn, Ivy!" He turns a bit, nodding to Barbie. "I do believe you have competition." Chuckling, he winks, turning back to her, running a hand through thick dark hair.

Ivy dips with a giggle, putting out her hands, and gives him a big red-lipped smile. "Why thank you, but I already have a date." Turning around, she puts out a hand.

A black-gloved hand grips around hers, and a shorter bit of curves emerges in a nice wrapping of shiny black leather from neck to toes. Her heels dig into the gravel. Bright silver zipper open to the middle of her stomach. Reaching a hand up to her black mask, she adjusts her cat ears, flipping her black hair.

Mr. Skeleton Man whistles. "I always knew there was a thing between Ivy and Selina. Mmm, mmm, mmmm..." Shaking his head, he turns to Barbie.

Barbie shifts her weight over the rocks, crunching them around, and eyes her nails.

Selina drops her whip, lunging her claws at him with a playful hiss. "And don't you get any ideas about a threesome, mister, um..." Stepping away from the car, she twirls her hand through the air.

Mr. Skeleton Man turns sharp on his heels, pointing behind him. "Oh, the other quite lovely lady has named me Mr. Skeleton Man, and I do so like it." Turning back, he smirks, putting a hand to his chest.

At that moment, the fourth limo door opens, and a massive black boot slams out on the gravel, pushing the rocks to the side. A large red hand grips the top edge of the door, gripping tight, and the limo creaks as its weight shifts. The next part to emerge is slicked black hair, broken and filed down red horns, and a lit cigar jutting out from a red smirk. Taking a few steps forward, he slings a giant rock fist into the driver's shoulder with a grunt and adjusts his khaki trench coat.

Barbie's eyes widen, and she squeals, biting her bottom lip.

Selina slings her whip at his foot, letting it crack loud, and everyone jumps. "Nice choice, Red, but DC is better." Grinning, she winks at him, coiling her whip, and puts it on her hip.

Red sniggers, pulling the cigar from his teeth. "Thanks, honey, but like my publishers, I prefer the dark horses." Moving towards them, the tail skitters and bounces over the rocks, rolling them around.

They all snigger and giggle until the next door opens, and everyone turns to the car.

A shining red dress shoe hits the rocks with the other close behind. Jolting from the car, a slight blur of yellow, red, and white swirls forward in a bit of a waltz until it all stops, pointing a finger at Ivy. Standing tall, he swipes a white hand through long thick red hair, giving her a smile through smudged red makeup. Winking through smeared black eye shadow, he puts out a hand and bows to her. His dingy red and white striped sleeve rises up his arms a bit, revealing the butt of a knife.

Everyone moves back a few steps, letting out stifled yelps.

Red stands tall, bowing out his large chest, and points a rock finger at him. "Hey, McJoker, lay off, ya creepy asshole." Taking a step towards him, he balls his fists, glaring at him.

McJoker stands tall, leaning back a bit, and puts out his hands to either side as he lets out a shrill laugh. "I'd love to, big guy, but you see, the thing is…" He pauses, locking onto each of them for a split second. "I just don't want to!" Going into another dance, he hops around and lets out kooky laughs.

Red takes a few more steps, grabbing McJoker's throat, and lifts him in the air while Barbie lets out a squeal. "You're freakin' out the ladies, dude. Cut it the fuck out." Winking, he drops him to the gravel.

McJoker coughs, choking out a laugh, and gets to his feet. "Fine, I was just following the rules." Running the tip of his tongue along the edge of his teeth, he smooths his hair back and adjusts his yellow vest.

Selina smirks, sniggering. "Good one, Red." Sniggering more, she leads them towards Barbie.

The next car door opens, and they all turn.

A pair of tan boots jut out, a set of hands gripping the upper edge of the door frame, and a dark-skinned guy swings out, landing hard on the gravel. His short khaki shorts grip tight to his thighs, ass, and crotch, riding up as he walks. Grabbing the collar of his dark brown state trooper jacket, he flings it forward, letting his fingers fan at them all.

The girls giggle, grinning at him, and the guys groan as they roll their eyes and shake their heads.

Adjusting his aviator sunglasses, he strokes his black moustache and then eyes Barbie. "Well, hello, Mrs. Doll." Flashing her a bright white smile, he blows her a kiss.

Barbie smirks. "Sorry, honey, I don't like guys who look better in booty shorts than me." Giggling, she shifts her weight with her hands on her hips. "And I think that's what I'll call you. Mr. Booty Shorts." Nodding a few times, she pats at her hair, rolling her tongue along her mouth.

Mr. Booty Shorts puts his hands on his hips, shifting his weight a lot. "Well, ma'am, I've been called a lot worse." Letting out an overly exaggerated breathy laugh, he turns to the others.

The next door opens, drawing everyone's attention.

Out comes a shining metallic silver petite cyborg with spikes jutting out over every curve, short bleach-blonde hair in two short wavy pigtails, and a silver face mask that would stop any man's heart. Moving towards them, the gears in her joints zip and zush as if she's actually made of mechanical parts.

McJoker slaps the back of his hand against Red's chest, cutting his eyes up at him, and addresses her. "Well, well, well… What have we got here. A nice little Robodolly." Sniggering, he steps up to her, running the back of his fingers over her cheek.

Rearing back a fist, Robodolly punches him in the gut, cocking her head as he hits the ground, and grins, speaking in an altered voice. "In your dreams, happy meal man." Stepping over his balled-up state, she zushes her way to the others.

McJoker flings his head back, red hair slinging about, and he laughs. "Oh, sweetie, almost as good as my little Harley back home." Laughing louder, he gets to his feet.

Another car door opens.

Out step faded black dress shoes, grey tweed dress pants,

brown plaid vest, and a blue button-up with the sleeves rolled. He tips a grey tweed golf hat, adjusting his gun and holsters, and loosens his black tie a bit.

Everyone stares.

Stroking his thin black beard, he eyes everyone and nods. "Evenin', gents, ladies." Grabbing the brim of his hat, he tips it to each lady. "So, what's the hubbub, bub?" Putting out his hands, he takes a few dipping steps towards them all.

Ivy laughs, looking him over. "What're you, some sort of cop?" Crossing her arms, she smirks with a snigger.

Mr. Skeleton Man chuckles, nodding. "Yea, he's... Casablanca." Chuckling again, he pats Casablanca on the shoulder. "That gun real?" Locking eyes with him, he takes the silence as a no and leads him towards the house.

Casablanca follows, eyeing Barbie a bit too long.

Barbie bites her bottom lip, eying him back for as long if not longer.

The next limo opens.

Out slides a light-skinned grime-covered female, tan boots grinding the gravel as she makes her way towards them. Flinging a long black braid off her shoulder, she puts her finger-less-gloved hands on her hips, scraping her nails over the leather weapon belt sitting in the loops of her tight army-green booty shorts. The weapons' straps press into her flexing thighs as she moves. Scratching at her collarbone, her fingers run over the dingy grey tank below empty black gun holsters.

Turning around sharp, Mr. Skeleton Man moves between Red and McJoker, putting his arms around their shoulders. "Damn, if one more hot-ass chick steps out of a limo, I may just have to flip a coin as to who I'll do first. But I have to say, Mrs. Croft has a good chance at first. Or would I want her last?" Smacking his lips, he chuckles with the both of them, patting their shoulders.

Lara smirks, black smudges stretching, and steps up to him, grabbing at his chin, and squeezes hard. "If your dick comes anywhere near me, you'll come to miss it sooner than you can kiss me good bye." Patting his cheek, she puckers a kiss at him, and walks off towards Ivy and Selina.

Mr. Skeleton Man snarls, spitting at the ground, and brushes off his suit. "Bitch." Rolling his tongue along his mouth, he turns away from her.

The last limo door opens, and everyone gets still and quiet.

A knee-high flappy black boot pushes out and hits the rocks. Out comes a tall, tanned figure in brown and red striped pants and a frilly white shirt. Long black hair under a red scarf tied tight around his head. A big-brimmed black hat with skull and crossbones sits atop it all, shadowing a black leather eyepatch. With the smudged black good eye, he looks them over before turning around with a hand out.

A slender pale hand slips into his, gripping tight, and a set of pale legs swings out the door. Bare feet hit the gravel. Shimmering blue scales and bright white bones shine through missing chunks of skin in her legs, leading up to a fishnet skirt. Seashells dangle on the netting, encircling her hips, and two large shells cover her large pale breasts. Gills protrude from her neck, with more scales and bone shining through her shoulders and arms. Piercing yellow eyes move toward everyone, and she smiles bright white fangs at them.

Barbie's mouth hangs open. "Ok, Little Mermaid and her Pirate Eric are the best costumes by far." Slicing her hand through the air, she scoffs, shaking her head at them.

Little Mermaid giggles. "You're sweet, Barbie, but from where I stand, we all look pretty damn awesome."

As each of them reaches the top step to the porch, an animatronic butler greets them, asking for ID and invitation. Once they put their drivers licenses and invites on his tray, he burns them to ash.

All twelve of them.

Entering the house, they all look around, marveling at the disgustingly awesome decorations. The strobe light gives everything around them a choppy and disjointed feel, as if every moment needs reassurance. Creepy sounds come from every direction. Animatronic hands reach out, grabbing different parts of them, making them scream and jump at different intervals.

Mr. Skeleton Man laughs. "Is this all? This is weak!" He lets out a shrill chuckle.

Barbie slams the back of her hand into his arm. "Cut it out, Skelly, don't you know that's like saying it can't get any worse?" She glares bright blue eyeshadowed eyes at him. "You'll jinx us." Gritting her teeth, she lets out a high-pitched squeal.

Mr. Skeleton Man chuckles, slipping an arm around her waist. "You can always cling to me, sweet Barbs." Winking, he pinches her ass, making her jump.

Barbie swings her hands at him more.

Skelly feigns defense, putting up an elbow, and laughs.

Rounding the corner to their right, they enter a room full of fog. In the cloud of white, they lose sight of each other for a moment, calling out and flinging hands through the air in hopes they hit someone. Following the echo of footsteps, they each find a black door, filing through it into a dining room of sorts.

Tall, oversized mushrooms. Massive blades of grass. Gigantic butterflies hanging overhead or sitting on the mushrooms. A huge to-scale caterpillar lays on the top of the biggest mushroom head across the room. Its eyes move back and forth, as if watching their every move.

Everything is coated in glitter and bright fluorescent paints on black with large over-the-top fixtures holding blacklights that fill the room with a blueish purple glow. Taking note of their costume color changes, they then turn their attention on the whimsically decorated room.

Skelly moves towards the long dining table dressed in a thick white tablecloth, winding florals, teacups galore, and expensive-looking over-the-top dinnerware. Picking up a gold-plated name plaque, he sniggers.

The others move toward him.

Turning to them, Skelly holds it up. "Zombie Mermaid?"

He glances around at them. "I wonder who that could be?" Arching an eyebrow, he cuts his eyes at each of them and grins.

Little Mermaid steps forward, snatching the name plate with a smirk, and slams it down, taking her seat. "Apparently we have designated seating." She shrugs, lacing her fingers, and rests her elbows on the table. "I suggest you find yours." Glaring at him, she leans back in her chair, crossing her arms.

The others chuckle and giggle, dispersing, and find their name plates.

Skelly sniggers, mumbling with a grin, "Uppity bitch." Finding his name plate, he ends up sitting across from her. "Who is this owner? And why are they so bougie to use gold-plated name cards?" Holding up his name plate, he winks at Little Mermaid with a quick pucker kiss.

Little Mermaid rolls her eyes, huffing, and looks off to her right, and runs her tongue along her teeth.

Skelly rolls his eyes at her, reaching forward. "Even the glasses have cards." He picks one up. "'Drink me'?" Pphhfffting, he sniggers, putting the card back on the table.

Lara glances around, holding up her name plate between a couple fingers. "What I wanna know is how they knew what we would call ourselves." She locks eyes with Selina and Red. "I never filled out a persona questionnaire." Shrugging, she sets the name plate down.

The others' eyes widen. They nod, and mumbling ripples over the table.

Barbie shrugs, tapping pink nails on her chin. "That's actually pretty damn creepy." Grimacing, she flings herself back in her seat, crossing her arms, and pulls her tube top down a bit.

The guys shift in their seats, eyeing her, and smirk to themselves.

All except Casablanca, who rubs his fingertips along his mouth, looking around the room.

At that moment, a creaking and shrieking comes from far off.

Barbie lets out a squeal, searching the room, and the others jump, pushing back in their seats.

Casablanca grips the table, searching the neon for an exit sign.

A black square descends at the head of the table, switching on to white noise static, and then a mock version of the Saw puppet appears on the screen.

Everyone lets out sighing laughs, relaxing a bit, and faces the television.

Casablanca releases his grip on the table's edge but remains braced to run.

The little puppet opens and closes its mouth, letting out an obviously masked and warped voice. "Good evening." It pauses, turning its head back and forth as if looking them over. "Tonight is a special event. You twelve have been specially selected to participate in Sykes Manor's first ever overnight competition. The rules are simple. Stay in your personas without deviation. Stay within the house or you forfeit. And whoever sees tomorrow's sunlight wins. Enjoy your last dinner and dessert." It pauses, looking them over once more. "Good luck." Letting out a high-pitched maniacal laugh, it shakes a bit, and then the television cuts off, ascending to the ceiling again.

Everyone turns back to each other, eyes wide, eyebrows up, and mouths gaping.

Barbie and Ivy shift in their seats as if unable to get comfortable again.

Red slams his hands on the table, making everything shake, clink, and rattle. "Well, the TV puppet said we'd be eatin', and I'm starvin'." He glances around, craning his neck. "Where's the food?" Puffing a bit, he breathes smoke out through his nose.

At that moment, a clicking, popping, and humming fills the room. From a corner, a black curtain splits, and a line of serving trays makes its way along a track to them. The silver glints purple and blue as they make their wobbling way to the table, stopping between each seat to their lefts.

In front of each set of covered plates is a name card with 'Eat Me & Enjoy' below their names.

In a clank-filled silence, each of them picks up their plate, putting the covers on the trays, and sets them on the dining ware.

Red glares down at a bowl full of chili and sniggers. "These people thought of everything. Damn. They even knew my favorite meal." Grinning, he dives on in, shoveling his spoon into his mouth.

The others glance around at the assorted and specifically prepared meals for each persona. Watching Red scarf down his chili, they all poke and prod their food until they each take that first hesitant bite.

Casablanca hesitates most. "Don't you guys think this is a bit weird?" He rests his wrists against the table, cutting his eyes around at each of them. "It's almost as if they knew exactly what we would dress as. And they make food catered specifically for us?" He shakes his head, pushing his plate forward. "It's a bit suspicious to me." Crossing his arms, he has to adjust his holsters.

Little Mermaid giggles, bringing her fork to her mouth. "Maybe they spied on us to up the creep factor." Grinning, she bounces her eyebrows, putting the fork in her mouth with another giggle, and speaks with her mouth full. "Oh, come on. I'm kidding." Swallowing, she rests her chin on a fist. "Do you really think they would go through that much trouble? Jeez." Furrowing her eyebrows, she leans back, sipping the water from her glass.

Barbie lets out a giggle. "Does sound pretty unlikely when you say it like that." Shaking her head, she puts a dainty forkful of chicken in her mouth.

Casablanca eyes them both, flitting a weak smirk, and shifts in his seat. "Yea, unlikely." Getting quiet, he eyes his plate of tagine with a small snarl.

The rest of them eat and chat away until their plates are mostly cleaned.

After several minutes of everyone not eating, a beeping rings through the room.

Everyone stops talking, glancing around the room again.

A neon, hand-painted sign glows across the room near another black curtain.

Ivy lets her words out on a breath. "Chocolate room." Licking her lips, she turns to everyone. "Dessert must be served." Grinning, she shrugs a shoulder, grabbing Selina's hand.

Rising from their seats, they all move through the curtain.

CHAPTER EIGHT

Pulling the curtain back, they file through two at a time.

The overpowering scent of sugar and sweets greets them.

Candles glow, scattered around the room in large melting clumps.

Lights flash.

Thunder rumbles.

Birds caw, wings flapping, and they move from high draping black branches overhead.

Barbie looks up, curling her lip. "If I get shit on, I'll be fucking pissed." She eyes the ceiling, running her hands over her skirt and thighs.

A cackling come from their left, and Barbie jumps, putting a hand to her chest. Letting out a breath, she kicks at the glowing pumpkin heads surrounding the archway she's under. The wheat stalks sway and rustle from the pressure and wind she creates.

Mr. Skelly steps up, speaking low in her ear. "Don't worry, Barbs, I'll keep you safe." Laughing through his nose, his breath moves her hair as he leans in to kiss her neck.

Barbie puts her perfectly manicured nails to his forehead,

pushing them apart, and scoffs. "As if, flimsy bag of bones." Removing her fingers, she flits him her most sarcastic grin and moves forward.

Selina and Ivy pass, and Selina pats the skeleton man's shoulder.

Skelly snarls, adjusting his lapels, and pats over his tux, moving farther inside.

Everyone marvels at the massive waterfall across the room leading down to a wide river running the length of the room towards a blackened archway. The splashing fills the room, humming over the rest of the sounds around them.

Small towers of jack-o-lanterns and pumpkin vines swirl out in places, glowing yellow and orange. Their vines on the floor wriggle and writhe over the dead sod.

Twisting and spiraling black trees reach out at them, as if handing them delectable sweets.

Small bushes of black thorny stems offers up edible flower heads of red, black, and white roses.

A cluster of rocks with bright white grins surrounds a jack-o-lantern tower with small cupcakes sitting on a table in the middle.

Black, red, and white lollipops sit scattered throughout the room.

Ivy steps up to a tree, pulling a small flat brown round from the limb, biting into it, and her eyes roll back as her lids flutter. "Mmmm, it's chocolate!" She turns sharp toward everyone. "It's a dark chocolate tart. Has a bit of a zing to it too." Eyes wide, she takes bite after bite until it's nothing more than melted sludge on her fingertips sliding from between her red lips.

Everyone grins, moving closer to the trees, and pulls down their own delectable sweet.

Chewing on a red licorice, Barbie moves towards the cakes near the smiling rocks and leans down towards the table.

One after the other, the teeth chatter, making the rocks

wobble, and they all let out high-pitched laughs into a chorus of creepy giggles.

Barbie jumps back, putting her nails to her teeth, and squeals. "Oh, holy hell!" Stumbling back a few steps, she bumps into Casablanca.

Casablanca puts out his hands, gripping her elbows, and flits a grin at her as he puts her straight. "It's okay, they won't bite." He points at them, swirling his finger. "See, they're on a motion sensor." As the last word escapes his lips, they stop, and he waves his hand in front of one, making them start up again.

Barbie giggles, grabbing a cupcake from the table, and holds it up to her smirking face. "Well, look who's the detective." Holding her smirk, she swipes a finger through the icing, licking it from her finger with a slight moan.

Casablanca's eyes widen, and he swallows hard, letting out a breathy laugh as he glances at the floor. "It was no problem." Tapping his fingers over his lips, he watches her wink and lick icing straight from the cupcake.

Barbie grins, sliding her hand over his shoulder as she moves on to a different place, tossing the cupcake to the ground.

Casablanca rubs the back of his neck, swiping the toe of his shoe over the dead grass, and chuckles to himself, watching her walk away.

Across the way, Red scarfs down several limbs' worth of chocolate tarts.

Ivy joins him at a tree, pulling off her own tarts, while holding a few cupcakes as well.

The two of them eat their fill, giggling and stumbling about.

The others mill about, tasting a few sweets, mostly staring at the dark brown-looking river.

Casablanca passes a corner, and a hand grabs his shoulder, pulling him backward as he lets out a slight yelp until a hand covers his mouth, and a giggle hits his ear.

Skelly watches him stumble back around the corner. Glancing

around, and no one watching, he moves towards them, keeping a distance, and chews on a red licorice.

Turning around, Casablanca comes face to face with a grinning Barbie. Giggling, she pulls him farther into the corner, wrapping her arms around his neck, and plants a hard kiss on his lips. Raising his eyebrows with a slight grunt, he walks her back to the wall, running his hands up her back.

Barbie lets out a light giggle as she bumps into the wall and moves her fingers over his beard to his chest, gripping the holster straps, and pulls him closer to her.

Skelly stands behind a partition, peeking through a hole, and watches the two of them.

Casablanca presses against her body, kissing along her jaw and neck, and slips his fingers under the edge of her tube top.

No bra.

On the other side of the room, Ivy and Selina exchange fingerfuls of whipped cream and meringue.

Selina glances around at everyone preoccupied with their sweets. Placing her hands on Ivy's shoulders, she walks her backwards into different corner.

Ivy opens her mouth in protest, but before a word escapes, Selina's lips are on hers. Letting out a small squeal, she leans into it, sliding her fingers down Selina's back, and grabs her ass, bringing her to her tip toes.

Selina giggles, taking off her gloves, and massages Ivy's breast. Slipping the other hand between her legs, she moves a few fingers back and forth under the clasp of her body suit. She grins at Ivy's light moans, pressing a finger past the crotchless stockings and into her, licking her neck.

Ivy lets out a loud moan, biting her bottom lip in an attempt to quiet herself despite the thunderous splashing background noise. Tugging down on Selina's zipper, she pulls the suit aside, cupping and massaging her breasts. Tugging the zipper to its end, she glances around for spies. Everyone preoccupied, she turns them around, swiping decorations from a short pillar, and puts Selina on it.

In the middle of the room, Booty Shorts walks to the edge of the bank, peering into the river. "Hey, guys!" He turns towards the remaining contestants. "Anything off about this river to any of you?" Putting a hand on his hip, he points a thumb over his shoulder towards the churning dark liquid.

The others glance his way but stay where they are.

Booty shorts turns back to the river, mumbling to himself. "Weird. Is it chocolate? Wine? It really fucking dark." He stoops, but Red stumbles past him, giggling a bit too much for a guy his size.

Back on the other side of the room, Casablanca has Barbie's top pulled down and her skirt around her waist. His pants hang around his thighs, and he holds up one of her legs, thrusting and grunting.

Barbie fights the urge to let out loud moans, taking in sharp breaths, and lets her mouth hang open. Biting her bottom lip, she lets out a light squealing moan. Grabbing at his hair, she pushes his head down.

Skelly strokes himself, keeping an eye out for the others while watching the two of them, and takes a bite of his licorice.

Letting out an obligatory grunt, Casablanca puts her legs on his shoulders, raising her up, and licks her until she lets out a screech and her thighs squeeze against his head. Leaning back, he pulls her from his shoulders, turning her around. Spreading her legs, he rubs himself over her for a second before thrusting back inside.

Barbie stifles a moan, gripping at the wall in front of her.

Skelly watches how her breasts press against the blackness of the wall, tan skin and hot pink making her stand out, and he strokes harder, taking another bite of his red licorice.

In the middle of the room, Red stumbles about more.

The others watch him, arching their eyebrows, and shake their head.

Red gets close to the edge of the bank, and Booty Shorts grabs his shoulders, standing him as straight as possible. "What's going on here, buddy? You ok?" He searches his face, taking a few steps forward, and does his best to back Red away from the bank.

The others move their way, mumbling to themselves.

Across the room, Ivy's tongue moves over Selina, dipping in and out, and rolls over her clit in a frenzy.

Selina moans, covering her mouth, and grips the pillar, digging her nails into it. Pulling Ivy's chin up, she grins, sliding from her perch, and has Ivy sit. Unclasping her body suit, Selina swipes over her slowly, flicking her tongue over her clit.

Ivy lets out a short and low moan, watching her every move, head lightening.

Reaching to her hip clip, Selina unbuttons it, letting her whip fall loose. Turning it around, she hands the grip to Ivy.

Grinning, Ivy nods, licking her lips, and grabs Selina's hand over the grip as she continues to lick over her clit. Raising the whip handle, she presses it to her red lips, rubbing over them.

Selina pushes harder, and Ivy opens her mouth, sticking out her tongue, and rolls it over the black silicone until it's as wet as she is.

Bringing the grip down, Selina rubs it over Ivy, rolling it along the clit, and then thrusts it inside her.

In and out.

In and out.

In and out, gaining in speed and power.

Tongue flicking her clit over and over.

Ivy jolts, stifling a moan midway, and arches her back, gripping the pillar so hard one of her fake green nails pops off. Jolting a bit more, she lets out a short scream, tensing her whole body, and a stream of white surges from her, coating Selina's lips and chin.

Selina lets out harsh laughs, lapping her up.

DEATH INVITES IN GOLD

Ivy jolts a couple more times, relaxing on the pillar, and her head swims.

Red throws Booty Shorts's hands off his shoulders, stumbling a few steps, and slurs his words. "Geh the fuff ov me, I nanna go sfimmin'." Giggling again, he takes a few steps towards the river.

Lara and Pirate Eric grab at his shoulders from behind, doing their best to keep him on the shore.

McJoker joins them, pushing against his chest with Booty Shorts.

Back in the other corner, Casablanca massages Barbie's breast, giving one last deep stroke before grunting as he jolts a few times, and Barbie lets out a loud moan.

Mr. Skeleton releases onto a nearby black curtain, wiping himself with it, and takes the last bite of his red licorice, walking off toward the others as he adjusts himself.

Moving from behind the partition, Barbie adjusts her skirt and tube top, attempting to smooth her hair. Clearing her throat, she wipes at her mouth, glancing around the room.

Casablanca rounds the corner, holding his hat, and tucks in the tails of his shirt. Shifting his hat over his head, he swipes over his mouth, smacking his tongue against the roof of his mouth with a grin. Looking up, he catches the commotion at the river's edge and halfway jogs to them.

Selina and Ivy appear not long after, and Selina gets one glove back on, glancing to her left.

Ivy sways a bit, putting her fingers to her lips. "I don't think I should've had so many tarts." Her cheeks puff up, and she stifles a gag.

Selina turns to her, putting a hand on her shoulder, and opens her mouth to speak, but a commotion stirs with Red.

Red flails his arm, pushing everyone aside. "Geh the fuff ofvme! I seh, I'ma goin' sfimmin'!" With staggering steps, he makes his way to the edge.

Casablanca reaches them, stretching out a hand, and grabs the belt of Red's trench coat.

Red stumbles, boot sliding over the bank's edge, and he turns part way around.

Casablanca tugs at the belt, lifting the coat towards him, and the buckle catches in the right loop.

Red turns all the way, pulling the belt from Casablanca's grip, and falls backwards with his arms out and a slight yelp.

.

CHAPTER NINE

Everyone screams and yells, putting out their hands, wiping their faces, or covering their mouths.

Casablanca puts his hands on his head.

Red falls hard into the river, spraying those at the bank's edge, and sinks below the bubbles and waves.

Casablanca, Booty Shorts, and McJoker turn away from the spray, but can't escape, sides and backs getting soaked.

Selina pets Ivy, stroking her hair, and watches her fight against vomiting.

Covering her mouth, Ivy runs to the river and pukes.

Everyone else watches the bubbles where Red fell in.

He's not coming back up.

Casablanca eyes the stains left behind on his sleeve and forearm, mumbling, "What's this?" Turning his arm over, he brings it to his nose. "Is that?" His eyes widen, and he falls on his hands and knees at the bank's edge.

Another round of splashing fills the room.

Selina screams, dropping to the edge with her hand in the liquid. "No! Paulina!" Lying on her stomach, she slaps her hands through, splashing and grabbing for Paulina.

Casablanca turns to Selina. "It's blood! It's a goddamned river of blood!" Eyeing the others, he plunges a hand into the blood, feeling around.

Robodolly steps towards him, fake voice shaking. "What do you mean it's blood? And why isn't Red coming back up?" She points a shaking finger towards the dead grass at her feet.

Casablanca ignores her, doing his best to search his hands through the churning red wine in front of him.

Selina continues her scrambling search, getting blood everywhere. "Paulina! You can't do this to me! You can't leave me!" She scoots herself closer, plunging her hands deeper into the moving red goop.

McJoker moves to Selina, searching the darkness before him.

Lara and Robodolly stand next to him, doing their best to make out ripples or bubbles.

Booty Shorts, Pirate Eric, and Little Mermaid watch next to Casablanca.

As they all search the flowing goop, ripples form in the middle, and Red bursts through, sending blood everywhere. Closed eyes and open mouth coated in blood and slime, he takes a ragged gasp, falling back into the dark abyss.

Selina screeches. "I've got her! I've got Paulina!" Managing to get on her knees, she grips tight with both hands.

Paulina's hand emerges, but Selina's grip slips and slides over her saturated skin. She attempts to readjust, dropping Paulina a few inches.

McJoker moves to her, reaching into the red, and moves his hands around until he grabs something. Pulling up, he and Selina manage to get Paulina's head to the surface.

Hair plastered to her face, she opens her mouth for air only to sputter and gag on bloody hair.

Casablanca turns around, searching for a long and strong object. Landing on the vines to the pumpkin towers, he moves for them, pulling the vines lying still on the floor. Coiling them around his shoulder and elbow, he races back to the bank.

Red flails, flinging his arms, and slings blood in all directions.

Casablanca drops the coil to his hand, unraveling a few feet. "Okay, Red! I'm throwing you a rope! Do your best to grab it! I'll do my best to make that easy!" Holding tight to the coil, he swings it a few times before flinging it out towards Red.

The vine falls around Red's shoulders, curling around his neck. He flails, grabbing for it, but keeps falling under.

Selina and McJoker have difficulty holding Paulina above the surface with the small current, her weight, and her slick skin slipping below their fingers. In one swift motion, their grips fail, and she falls prey to the moving depths below.

Selina falls forward, plunging her hands into the red. "No, no, no, NO!" In her frantic state, she lets out a sob, continuing to slap at the water, and screeches.

McJoker takes a few backward steps, putting bloody hands on the top of his head, shaking it, and breathes deep and fast.

The others cover their mouths, watching both Red and Paulina fall under.

A few ripples.

Fewer bubbles.

Casablanca pulls the vine towards himself, readying for another toss. "This can't be happening." Coiling the vine, he braces for the toss.

Mr. Skeleton grabs his arm, squeezing a bit, and locks eyes with him. "There's no point. They're gone. There's no way they could fight that current. Not in their costumes, and not with how thick it all is." Shaking his head, he turns towards the now placid river, save the churning from the falls.

Casablanca jerks his arm, slinging the vines across the grass. "Damn it!" Without thinking, he wipes his mouth, pulling his hand away, grimacing, and huffs.

Selina sits in the grass, hugging her legs, and ugly-cries into her knees, rocking back and forth.

Lara, Barbie, and Robodolly crouch on either side of her, rubbing her shoulders.

McJoker stands still, staring into the void between him and the grass, fingers curling into his hair.

Little Mermaid and Pirate Eric hold onto each other, staring at everyone.

Booty Shorts runs towards a tree, vomiting over the roots.

Casablanca turns towards everyone, looking them over, and scratches the back of his neck.

At that moment, a red light flashes across the room, and a bridge extends over the river.

Booty Shorts stumbles towards the group, holding his stomach. "There's a bridge." He wags a finger in its direction. "Maybe we should try to leave the room?" He shrugs, glancing around at everyone, and swallows hard with heavy breaths.

Barbie stands from behind Selina, glancing at the bridge, and glares at Booty Shorts. "How do we know it won't fall apart below us?" She points to it, taking a few wobbling steps towards him as her heels dig into the soft grass. "What if that was their plan? Drop us all in the river?" Taking heavy breaths, she stares at him, chewing the corner of her mouth.

Casablanca steps up to her, putting a hand to her back. "I don't think they would give us a way out if they just wanted us all to fall in at the beginning." He glances over everyone, sighing. "It's obviously a well-planned game." Snarling, he cuts his eyes behind him at the river. "And they lost." Turning back to everyone, he huffs. "We need to leave. Someone try the way we came through." He points to the black curtain.

Little Mermaid nods, removing herself from Pirate Eric, and makes her way to the curtain, pushing the fabric to either side. "It's closed!" She turns back to them. "There wasn't a door here when we passed through, but there is now, and it's locked." Eyes wide, she moves fast back to Eric.

Mr. Skeleton kicks a pumpkin. "Fuck, man! So we're forced to either sit in here and possibly die, or move forward and possibly die? Fuck this shit!" Shaking his head, he throws up his hands, turning away.

Selina lets out a shrieking sob, shaking.

Barbie puts her hands in her hair, turning in a circle.

Booty Shorts vomits into the river.

McJoker hasn't moved.

Mermaid and Eric hold onto each other.

Casablanca huffs, turning to Selina. "Can you walk? Or do you need help?" He moves to her, squatting, and searches her face beyond the mask.

Selina's eyes dart toward him, locking onto his with ferocity. "I just watched my girlfriend drown in a fucking river of blood, and you're asking if I can walk?" Lurching to her feet, she rushes him, pointing a finger in his face.

Casablanca falls back as the girls move away from her.

Selina holds her finger inches away from his face. "Paulina was the love of my life!" Hand shaking, she drops it, lip and chin quivering, and falls to her knees, sobbing.

McJoker jerks his attention to her, turning around. "You keep calling her Paulina." He glares at the back of her head.

Selina nods, sniffling.

McJoker glances at everyone. "I knew a Paulina back in high school." He watches her shoulders drop.

Selina sniffles again, turning her face to him, and takes off her mask. "I seriously doubt she's the same one." Letting out a whimpering laugh, she wipes the tears from her face.

McJoker squints, staring at her. "Miku?" His eyes widen, and he leans away.

Barbie jerks her head towards Miku. "Wait, what?" She drops to her knees with a hand on Miku's shoulder. "Miku, is that really you?" Grabbing her chin, she turns Miku's faces back and forth.

Miku jerks her chin from Barbie's hand. "Do I know you two?" Arching an eyebrow, she eyes them.

Barbie rolls her eyes, putting a hand to her cleavage. "It's me, Merrien, duh!" Shaking her head, she turns to McJoker. "Who are you, though?" Arching an eyebrow, she sneers at him.

RACHEL BROSS

McJoker chuckles a bit. "Blake... I'm a little surprised you didn't recognize me, but the makeup is pretty damn good." Sniffling, he shrugs a shoulder.

Barbie rolls her eyes again. "You always were a little shit, Blake." Scoffing, she stands, crossing her arms.

Casablanca shakes his head, getting to his feet, and puts out his hands to them. "Wait a minute, do all of you know each other?" Arching an eyebrow, he moves a squinting gaze over everyone.

Robodolly nods, raising her hand. "I know them." She cuts off the machine altering her voice. "It's me, Bubbles." She flits her gaze at each of them.

Casablanca points to Booty Shorts. "And you?" Holding his gaze on him, he crosses his arms.

Booty Shorts holds his stomach, nodding. "Yea, I dated Bubbles in high school." He turns to her, giving her a nod, and wiggles his fingers.

Bubbles squints. "Houston?" Taking a step closer, her eyes widen.

Casablanca turns to Eric and Mermaid. "And you two? What're your real names?" He puts out a hand to them.

They glance at each other, shaking their heads.

Mermaid tightens her grip on him. "I don't know any of you. My name's Robin." She shrugs a shoulder.

Eric shakes his head. "I'm Jessie, her boyfriend." Shrugging, he puts up his free hand.

Casablanca sighs, rubbing his face, turning to Lara and Skelly. "Well?" Tapping his chin, he eyes them.

Skelly nods. "Yea... hey, guys. Tyler." He waves to them, shrugging his lips, and rolls his eyes to the floor.

Lara frowns. "Dorine. Hey." She grimaces, sucking in through her teeth.

Casablanca points a thumb at the river. "Do any of you have an idea of who Big Red was?" He glances at them each.

Tyler shrugs, throwing up his hands, and rests them on his

head. "I don't know, man." He paces. "If this is what I think it is, then that might have been Jeb." He stops moving, cutting his eyes around the group. "Fits the build, but it doesn't make sense." He shakes his head, eyeing Casablanca . "If they wanted us all here, they forgot Nathan." He glares at Casablanca , frowning.

Casablanca huffs, wiping over his mouth. "I have an idea of why." He flits his gaze at Tyler, dropping back to the floor. "I took his invitation." He drops his shoulders, letting his hand slap his thigh. "He died of an overdose after I entered us both into the contests with separate addresses." He locks eyes with Tyler. "He got in, so I took his ticket." Putting out his hands, he shrugs.

Tyler chuckles, shaking his head. "Of course, Nathan would skip out, as always." Shaking his head at the dead grass, he drops his hands from his head.

Miku giggles, letting it turn manic. "Paulina and maybe Jeb are dead, and you all are making introductions?" She points towards the river. "What the fuck is wrong with all of you?!" Her voice rises in pitch. "There are two dead people feet away from us, and you just want to chit chat over the fact that we all know each other?" She glares at their silent stares. "Who gives a fuck?! We need to get out of here and find the police!" Digging her fingers in her hair, she studies the floor. "I swear to God, I'm going to sue the shit out of the owner. Oh, they're going to wish I'd killed them." Letting go of her hair, she stalks the a few feet back and forth.

Casablanca takes a step towards her, stopping at her manic stare. "My name is Corey. I happen to be a cop." He bounces his gaze between her eyes. "If I make it out of here, you have my word I will make sure the killer is found and taken care of, but…" He glances at each of them. "For now, we need to get out of this room, and it looks like that's our only bet." Turning around, he puts out a hand to the bridge.

Robin cuts her eyes at Jessie, snarling, and shakes her head.

Jessie shrugs.

Nodding, everyone heads for the bridge.

CHAPTER TEN

M aking their way towards the red-lit skull archway, they move through the black curtain, coming to a quick stop as Corey puts out both hands to the sides. Everyone gawks at the hallway.

White faces line the walls. Each different. Each in pain. And each crying red.

Wailing.

Moaning.

Crying.

Anguish fills their path.

Miku steps up to one, touching the tears, and pulls her finger back, rubbing it against her thumb. "It's…" Sniffing it, her eyes widen. "It's real blood." Rubbing her hand over the wall, she snarls, stepping back from it.

Merrien fakes a gag, putting her hand over her mouth. "That's disgusting. I think I'm gonna vomit." Squeezing her eyes shut, she turns away from them, putting her face in Corey's shoulder.

Cutting his eyes around at everyone, he pulls her into a slight hug, patting her back.

Tyler sneers, rolling his eyes, and mumbles. "Get a room,

fuckers." Shaking his head, he turns face to face with one, eyeing it over. "Strange little things, aren't they?" He pokes it, and red fills the space. "The fuck?" He leans closer.

The mouth opens wide, and it cries out a shrill, unrelenting wail.

Tyler stumbles back, bumping into Dorine and Bubbles. "Fuck!" Twitching and jolting away from them, he bumps into the wall with a loud fwap.

Everyone glares at him.

Tyler shrugs, tugging at his tuxedo lapels, and shakes his head at them. "The fuck you all staring at?" Sucking his teeth, he shakes his head more, turning his gaze to the floor.

A fire erupts down the hall, drawing everyone's attention. The flame rise higher and higher towards the ceiling.

The hallway seems to extend farther than first thought with the new light.

Swallowing hard, Cory glances at the others while holding Merrien. "There's an exit sign just past that fire pit. I know the rules said if we leave we forfeit, but I think it's safe to say those rules were bullshit and if we stay we die. So, I say we make for the exit and do our best to find the highway we came in on." He locks eyes with each of them, nodding. "Agreed?" He watches them all nod, and he leans Merrien away from his shoulder, keeping his arm around her waist, and they all move forward.

As they make their way toward the fire pit, the moans, wails, and crying intensify, amplifying to the point most of them cover their ears.

Hugh and Dorine slow their pace, feet away from each other.

Jessie and Robin pass them to keep up with the others, and Robin glances over her shoulder at them before turning forward.

Person after person passes Hugh and Dorine.

Step after step, they slow down, both lagging behind.

Corey yells over his shoulder, but the faces are so loud, he can't hear his own voice. So instead he points ahead at the exit sign, and slings his head toward their right.

74

In the midst of the thunderous noise, Dorine and Hugh's steps fall hard and slow.

Hugh stumbles, grabbing at the wall, and leans his shoulder into it.

Dorine trips over her foot, scraping her nails over the wall, and falls to her knees, putting a hand to her chest.

No one turns around.

Both fight to breathe, opening and closing their mouths but neither getting air.

Before either of them realizes, they seize, muscles not wanting to move, mouths shut tight, and they fall to the floor, wide eyes staring at each other.

Bubbles holds her ears, glancing toward the door behind them, and a glinting catches her eye. Stopping in her tracks, she eyes the floor, finding the glint coming from Hugh's glasses lying feet from his unmoving body. Eyes widening, she takes in deep breaths, turning her gaze, and spies Dorine. Deeper, faster breaths, and then she lets out a blood-curdling scream that pierces through the noise.

Everyone stops moving, turning around.

The noises cease, but Bubbles's scream remains.

Merrien, Robin, and Miku's screams mingle into a chorus of high-pitched shrieks as they all come to face the two sets of blue lips, pale faces, and glaring glassed-over red eyes.

Corey pushes his way from the front toward the bodies and checks their pulses. Collapsing at Dorine's head, he wipes his face, letting it linger in his hand with a huff.

Bubbles sobs into Merrien's shoulder.

Miku stands there, staring, and hovers her shaking hands in front of her face.

Robin clings to Jessie, eyeing everyone.

Tyler bites his fist, turning in a quick circle, and then puts his hands on the back of his head. "Fuck!" Slinging his hands down, he shakes his head at the floor.

Blake squats, burying his face in both hands.

Corey yells out, slamming his fists into the wall, making the girls squeal.

At that moment, the fire pit falls, shrouding the room in darkness.

Everyone screams, becoming fully aware of new danger.

The wails return.

A strobe light flashes, chopping them in bright blue light.

They scramble into runs.

Corey does his best to yell over the noise, but it proves too great. Finding who he can, he moves them past the fire pit. Getting to a door, he pushes them all through, and it slams locked behind them.

All of them jump, turning around to it.

Miku glances around. "Where're the others?" Her eyes widen, breaths hastening, her voice rises two octaves. "Where the fuck are the others?" She grabs at the door, pulling and pulling to no avail.

Blake paces along the wall, hands on his head, eyes glazed.

Giving up, Miku slams her hands against the door, sobbing into it, and slides to the floor.

Corey steps up to her, resting a hand on her shoulder, and sighs. "I don't know. I did my best getting all of you to follow me, but maybe they'll find their own way out." Shrugging, he sighs again, wiping his face.

The quiet fills their ears as a green light floods the hallway.

One after the other, they all turn away from the door, facing an indistinguishable glow at the farthest end of the hall.

Merrien grabs hold of Corey's arm, gripping tight to his sleeve, and clings to him. "What is that?" Her grip tightens, nails digging into his skin through the fabric.

Miku and Blake join them, glaring at the glow, and tense.

Corey huffs, narrowing his eyes, and flexes his fists. "I don't know, but stay close and keep your eyes open for anything." Patting Merrien's hand, he squeezes and leads them forward.

The four of them move in a tight-knit group forward, looking around the corridor.

Corey glances from side to side.

No doors.

Nothing but straight black.

Turning forward, he comes face to face with the glowing figure, a grin spread across its misshapen face. He stops short, squeezing Merrien's hand still grasping tight to his bicep, and she squeals.

The glowing figure tips his top hat at them, then opens his mouth inhumanly wide, letting out a shriek loud enough to wake the dead before he barrels at them with his hands out.

Merrien lets out a shriek of her own in Corey's ear, turning her face into his shoulder, and braces.

Miku and Blake cling to each other, holding their breath as the apparition draws nearer.

CHAPTER ELEVEN

D own a different hall on the opposite side of the fire pit, Tyler bangs on a locked door. "Fuck! The door's locked!" Growling, he kicks at it a few times before running his fingers through his hair and turning around.

Robin clings to Jessie, glancing around the dark space. "Where are we?" Her fingers curl into his shirt, hard breaths making the collar ruffle.

Brenda rubs her arms, hugging herself. "Where did the others go?" She holds back sobs, staring at the floor. "What's going to happen to them?" She sniffles, turning her eyes up at Tyler.

Tyler steps up to her, pulling her into a hug. "We can't think about that right now, we need to find a way out of here." Stroking her back, he lets her wrap her arms around him, and he turns them from side to side.

Jessie looks around them, spying a flickering light. "Hey, there's a light down there." He eyes Tyler. "Maybe it's close to out?" He shrugs, looking down at Robin.

Tyler nods, letting go of Brenda, and stands tall. "Yea, or it leads to us dying. Fuck that." Snarling, he spits at the floor.

Jessie rolls his eyes. "Have it your way." He locks eyes with

Robin. "You wanna go check it out?" Rubbing her back, he waits for her to respond.

Robin moves her eyes over the floor, biting her bottom lip, and then turns up to him. "Yea, if there's any possibility it leads out, I want to take it." Nodding, she turns them to move.

Jessie glances at Tyler over his shoulder, giving him a shrug.

Tyler stands his ground, glaring at him.

Shrugging his lips, Jessie turns forward, leading Robin towards the light.

Tyler and Brenda watch the two of them get smaller and darker the farther away they walk.

Once they get to the light, the two of them enter a room, disappearing past the threshold.

Brenda turns up to Tyler.

Tyler huffs, rolling his tongue along his mouth. "What?" Huffing again, he glares at the pitch-black ceiling.

Brenda opens her mouth, only to clack it closed, and turns her attention to the light.

Groaning, Tyler rubs his eyes, pinching the bridge of his nose, and looks at her. "You want to follow. Why?" Shrugging, he shakes his head, flinging out his hands, and lets them slap his thighs.

Brenda chews her bottom lip, cutting her eyes to the floor. "Well, for one, they're not screaming." Flitting her gaze back up at him, she resumes chewing her lip.

Rolling his tongue along his mouth more, he hangs his head in defeat. "Fine, but if we die…" He points a finger at her, wagging it a bit, and then drops it at his side, shaking his head.

Brenda nods, turning forward.

Taking her hand, Tyler leads them towards the light.

Getting closer, the doorway widens, revealing those thick and wide clear plastic flaps you find in loading docks or slaughterhouses.

The light flickers behind them.

A dim, yellow light.

Tyler puts an arm between two of the flaps, pushing them apart. "Robin?... Jessie?... Hey, man, where you at?" Pulling Brenda along, he moves farther into the room.

Robin's voice comes from far off. "We're back here! This room goes on for a while."

Tyler cuts his eyes at Brenda. "Still wanna be in the room with light?" Cocking his head, he arches an eyebrow at her.

Brenda flits her eyes up at him, scrunching her eyebrows, and glances around.

Dingy white subway tile runs halfway up the wall to a grimy teal paint.

Red and brown smears cover the floor, trailing towards a drain in the middle of the concrete.

A bright chrome table with a small motor and crank sits bolted to the floor feet away. Shining clasps hang open at each corner.

Across from it sits a glinting clear plexiglass box with a metal inner wall and a small outside motor attached.

The two of them stand there, staring. Neither is willing to move, especially not first.

Jessie's voice come from the small archway at the back of the room. "Hey! You two coming back here or not?" His words trail off, and short giggles follow.

Tyler looks down at Brenda, arching an eyebrow, and shrugs.

Brenda chews her thumbnail, glancing back behind them, and whispers, "Maybe we should find another way out?" Nodding a few times, she looks up at him with her nail still between her teeth.

Tyler grins, laughing through his nose. "Finally, you say something smart." Putting an arm around her, he turns them to leave.

Without warning, yellow arms wrap around their shoulders. Black-gloved hands lace their fingers across their chests.

Brenda screams, scratching and grabbing at the thick black gloves.

Tyler does his best to struggle, almost succeeding in throwing the figure over his shoulder, but loses his footing in the slick trailing red. Falling back, the arms pull him backwards.

Before either of them realizes, they're shoved into the devices.

———

Back on the other side of the hall, a white apparition bursts through the wall to their left, hands out, and claws at them.

Miku squeals, getting the others' attention, and they all jump.

Merrien lets out another shriek, letting go of Corey, and sets out running in her stilettos.

The white apparition passes through the three remaining still.

Merrien glances over her shoulder at them, watching the apparition disappear. Turning around, she skids to a stop as the green one passes through her, and then her heel breaks, and she falls forward onto the cold hard tile floor. Her skin screeches as it skitters her to a halt.

The others rush to her, and Corey stoops to his knees, resting a hand on her shoulder. "You okay?" He helps her roll onto her side, glancing over her body.

Merrien blows her hair from her face, snarling up at him. "I hate this fucking place so much." Propping herself up better, she reaches for his shoulder, curling her fingers tight into the fabric.

Corey sniggers, glancing at the others, and grabs hold of her arms, helping her up on wobbling feet.

Merrien hobbles a bit, hopping and toeing around in her broken shoe. "The shits broke my shoe!" Reaching down, she takes it off, tossing the pair toward the door.

Scratching his beard, Corey holds a hand on the small of her back, cutting his eyes at the other two, and then turns to the floor. "We should keep walking. Try and find another door." Nodding to them, he maneuvers Merrien around, and they move farther along the hallway.

More apparitions move through the hall. Two of them dance together in Victorian-era clothing. Another white apparition lunges for them from the side.

Merrien squeals, grip tightening on Corey's arm.

Unbeknownst to him, Corey steps on a small black button in the floor.

A soft, slow clicking and clacking fills the corridor, growing in speed and volume.

One step.

Two steps.

Third step, a deafening clank fills the hallway, and the walls push together.

Everyone screams.

The hall narrows to the point everyone is single file.

Corey stands at the head of the line, hitting and pushing the walls as they slow their advance.

Merrien screams and cries, thrashing at the walls, and her bare feet slap the floor with each frantic stomp.

Miku falls to her knees, hands over her head, sobbing between her elbows.

Blake does his best to push the walls, shoes slipping over the slick floor.

A few loud clicks, and the walls stop moving.

They all look around, turning towards the ceiling and the floor before shuffling around towards each other in the shoulder-tight space.

Merrien's breaths hasten as she faces away from Corey towards Miku. "I – I can't… I can't, breathe! I've got to get out!" Her words come out rushed. "I can't! It's too small! There's not enough room!" Her breaths hasten more, pitch rising. "I need to get out! NOW!" Pushing into Miku, she attempts to plow over them towards the locked door.

Corey reaches for her, grabbing her fingers. "Merrien, wait! That door's locked!" Grabbing with both hands, he tugs her arm.

At that moment, the floor pulls out from below her.

Merrien screeches, swinging her free hand to Corey's wrist.

Seconds later, another bit of floor slides out from under Blake, and he drops.

Miku screeches, putting shaking hands in front of her mouth as his blood sprays over her and the walls around them.

The sound of his bones crunching between spinning claws fills the tight corridor, mingling with his yells and gurgling as the blades reach his lungs, filling them with blood. Red spurts from his mouth, hitting Miku in the face, and dribbles over his chin with each choke until he lowers, and his skull is crushed.

An eye pops out, bouncing on the claws before falling into a crack between them as they move towards each other.

CHAPTER TWELVE

The yellow figures disappear as fast as they came.

Brenda and Tyler are left alone, screaming and hollering and fighting against their confines.

The motors attached to the devices fire up. Whirring and humming fill the room.

Benda pushes her wrists and ankles against the tight metal cuffs, pressing the cloth into her skin.

The cuffs don't budge.

However, the table moves.

Brenda cranes her neck, glancing around the metal. "What the fuck is going on? Is this thing moving?" Squealing, she throws her head back into the gleaming silver, banging it over and over as she attempts to pull free.

Tyler grunts and groans, head protruding through the top of the box. "I'm a bit too preoccupied with my own problems right now." Opening his eyes, he glances her way. "But yes, the table is spreading apart from the middle." He takes in deep and harsh breaths, grunting as he pushes his feet against the walls of his box. "Mine is trying to press me into mush!" Holding his breath, he pushes again as the internal wall continues its advance.

The table stretches out more, stopping short with a sizeable gap between the pieces, and the cuffs move away from her on their own separate arms. They pull at her joints, drawing her arms above her head and pulling her legs out wide.

Brenda lets out a screech toward the ceiling, spit stringing between her teeth and lips, and then lets out a sob. "I'm sorry, Tyler! I'm so sorry!" Letting out another screech, her fingers jerk and spread wide.

The arms continue to pull her limbs away from her body. Her skin stretches. Breaths erratic. She cries.

Tyler grunts, still attempting to push at the inner wall of the box, and his words come out in huffs. "Don't... not your fault... Bubbles..." Letting out rapid breaths, he pushes and pushes against the power of the machine.

No matter how hard he pushes, the wall advances on him, and Tyler's knees meet the top panel of plexiglass. The wall keeps coming, pressing his toes towards his shins. Thighs against his stomach. His arms are pinned at his sides.

Tyler yells out.

Knees pushing upward into the plexiglass. Thighs pressing farther into his stomach.

Diaphragm.

Ribs.

A snapping.

Tyler screams, letting out a whimper. "Fuck! My ankles just broke! I just watched the blood spew." Leaning his face towards the ceiling, his tears flow into his ears, head lightening.

The wall continues to advance, pushing his feet farther into his shins.

Brenda screams again.

The arms pull her limbs farther and farther out.

Four pops fill their ears.

Brenda screams once more, letting it turn to sobs. "My joints just came out of their sockets!" She cries more, breaths manic, and her tears flow into her hair.

The arms continue to pull, stretching her skin.

Brenda wags her lightened head over the table, yellow light overhead swirling the room in a glow. "This thing is going to pull my limbs from my body." Sobbing harder, she strangles on her own saliva.

The arms click a few times, motor ramping up.

Tyler cries, listening to the rapid-fire cracking of Brenda's suit ripping at the seams as the fabric is pulled with her. Head lightening more, he watches her through blurry vision.

The wall presses his legs farther into him.

Two loud pops.

Tyler bursts into a sobbing yell. "My knees just busted." He swallows hard, spit flying from his lips with his next words. "I'm pretty sure the caps are tiny pieces now." Letting his head fall forward, he cries into the box, tears and spit mingling on the cold hard surface.

The wall continues to push into him, pressing his thighs into his ribs.

———

Merrien screams and squeals, clinging to Corey's sweating palm. Glancing down, she meets the heat of a large furnace.

Corey grunts, doing his best to pull her with his slipping grip, and strains his words. "Miku, it would be really nice if you could come help me." His face contorts as he manages to hold up her weight.

Merrien's feet swing feet above open flame. She picks them up, doing her best to move them away from the intense heat. The longer they dangle, the more her hot-pink nail polish softens, running over the sensitive skin of the tips of her toes. The soft bottoms of her feet redden, stinging and burning. She squeals more, kicking her feet, and adds to her already problematic weight.

Corey does his best to counter balance her heft with what little slipping grip he has. "Miku!" He glances at her staring at the grinder in front of her. "Damn it, Miku! I need your help!" His feet slip, and he falls forward a bit.

Merrien screams loud, hand slipping a good inch out of his grip.

The stench of her burning flesh surrounds them.

Feet blistered and black now, Merrien no longer kicks them. Her legs are next, reddening and blistering to her knees.

Miku turns around, hands still shaking, and she nods several times, making her way towards them. In her shocked state, she reaches down one second too slow.

Corey's grip slips one more time, and he's freed of her weight.

Merrien lets out a blood-curdling scream, falling the short distance into the flames below. Hair set ablaze, skin bubbling and charring, she reaches smoking fingers up to them. Her screams gargle to nothing. Falling still, the weight of her arms makes them crack, and they crumble to her chest.

Miku stifles a whimper, clamping her hands over her mouth, and all breath escapes her lungs.

Corey falls backwards, glaring at the gaping hole in the floor, and his breaths hasten. Propping his elbows on his knees, he folds a hand over the other, pressing them to his forehead, and rocks back and forth. Letting out a yell, he gets up and punches the wall.

Miku jumps at his outburst, dropping her hands to her sides, and stares at him. Her entire body shakes, loose strands of hair with it.

Turning around fast, Corey grabs her, pulling her close, and holds her tight as she cries into his chest.

The walls recede, floors closing, and the locked doors open.

Miku and Corey jerk their gazes toward the door.

————

Brenda eyes her restraints.

The arms let out one last click.

Tyler and Brenda lock eyes, tears streaming down their faces.

In the next instant, the arms jut from the table, pulling Brenda's limbs from her body.

They both scream as a spray of red coats the room.

As her body drains of blood, Brenda glances at her taken limbs, head falling back against the table, and she rolls it back and forth.

Tyler cries, watching red spurt from her and pool below the table.

The wall pushes harder into him. Red fills the box, soaking into his tux. He strains to breathe, wheezing in and out.

Tight.

Numb.

Heart racing, his head lightens more.

A clicking comes from the box, motor ramping up.

Tyler lets out a raspy gargling laugh, laying his head back, and stares at the ceiling.

One last click.

The wall smashes his legs into him. Crunching his hips, snapping his ribs, and puncturing his lungs, it presses his body flat against the back wall of plexiglass in a gush of red.

Tyler's head lurches forward. Deep red spews from his mouth. And a ragged gurgling escapes before his chin hits the box's surface, eyes glaring at Brenda on the table.

———

In the hallway, Robin and Jessie run toward Corey and Miku, skidding to a halt as they get close, and put their hands over their noses, stifling gags.

On instinct, Corey moves them away, putting Miku behind him. "Where did you two come from?" He eyes them. "And where are the other two?" He takes another step back, keeping his hands on Miku's arms.

Robin's bottom lip and chin quiver as she points behind her. "I don't know, but we heard a lot of screaming. We've been moving through hallway after hallway. Trying door after door." She lets out a sob. "This place is so fucking messed up." Leaning into Jessie, she clings to his shirt. "We just want to go home." Letting Jessie wrap his arms around her, she cries into his chest.

Jessie turns to them, stroking Robin's back. "We were with them in a slaughterhouse-looking room, but they never came to the back with us." He shrugs, shaking his head. "We kept walking. They never showed." He glances at the top of Robin's head. "Then we heard the screams. So many damn screams." Jerking his gaze up, he locks eyes with Corey. "That's when decided to try every door we came to, and that one was unlocked." Nodding behind him, he holds his eyes on Corey.

Corey eyes him over, nodding a few times. "We lost Merrien and Blake, too." Grabbing hold of Miku's hand, he turns partway towards her. "We need to get out of here, now." He nods behind himself, in the direction they were all headed before.

Jessie nods, turning him and Robin towards them, and they follow close behind.

CHAPTER THIRTEEN

The four of them reach the end of the hall, coming to a door labeled 'stairs.'

Corey turns to them, nodding to the door. "You think this could be a way out?" Arching an eyebrow, he glances at Miku shaking in his arm.

Jessie turns to Robin. "What do you think?" Shrugging, he furrows his eyebrows.

Robin chews her bottom lip, scrunching her face at the floor. "It could lead to the roof." She shrugs, shaking her head a bit. "If we can get up there, we may be able to find a way down and out." Nodding several times, she glances from Jessie to Corey.

Corey nods once, cutting his eyes at them for a second, and rubs over Miku's arm. "Okay, roof it is." Turning around, he pushes the door.

Creaking open, the hinges screech a bit as the heavy metal comes to a stop against the wall behind it. A dark set of stairs greets them, reeking of mold and mildew.

Corey glances down at the top of Miku's head, taking a dep breath, and leads the four of them upwards.

One flight.

Two flights.

Three.

Another door labeled 'roof.'

Sighing, Corey turns to them, arching an eyebrow.

Jessie and Robin scrunch their faces, shrugging.

Turning away, Corey reaches for the door.

Pushing it open, they all peer out at the moonlit rocks covering the roof.

At that moment, a large arm curls itself around Corey's throat.

Miku screams, falling from his grip.

Jessie struggles to keep Corey still.

A needle appears in the corner of Corey's eye. He looks to Miku in throes with Robin.

Robin grins from ear to ear, shoving a needle into Miku's neck, and drives the plunger of a syringe down until it's empty. Jerking the needle from Miku's flesh, she watches her stumble through the door and scramble over the rocks.

Corey continues to struggle, doing his best to keep away from the needle. He and Jessie fumble and stumble through the door, crunching and shifting over the rocks.

The two of them grunt and heave.

Jessie manages to get the needle into Corey's neck, pressing down on the plunger.

Robin lets out a grunting laugh as she follows Miku along the roof. "You thought you were so headstrong and perfect. You thought you could get away with anything, didn't you?" She laughs again, spitting at the rocks. "Well, you couldn't get away from me, now could you?" She watches Miku sway and stumble towards the roof's edge.

Corey gains some momentum and footing, grabbing hold of Jessie's arm, and flings him over his shoulder to the roof.

The rocks skitter and crunch below the new and unexpected weight.

Jessie tumbles and rolls over himself to a lobbing stop feet away.

Grabbing the syringe, Corey jerks it from his neck, throwing it to the ground, and presses his fingers into his flesh as he slams a foot over the plastic, cracking and grinding it into the small stones. Turning to his right, he watches Miku tripping over her feet near the roof's edge.

Robin walks beside her, bobbing and weaving with a sickening grin plastered on her face.

Corey moves toward them, steps heavier than before, and the roof sways a bit. "Miku, no!" His word slur a bit. "Youhl faw!" Shaking his head, he squeezes his eyes shut, then flutters them open, mumbling. "Bad idea." Turning to look over his shoulder, he stops.

Jessie's gone.

Shit.

Out of nowhere, a force hits Corey from the side, knocking him to the ground.

Jessie sits on top of him, curling both hands around Corey's throat, and presses down into his trachea.

Robin grunts out at them in excitement, turning back to Miku standing at the edge.

Miku wobbles, staring off at nothing in particular. Taking one more step, her boot shuffles over the stucco, ankle bending, and she twists. Eyes widening, she opens her mouth, but nothing comes out as she leans over.

Robin rushes to her, bending over, and watches Miku's descent to the gravel drive below.

A loud crunching fwack fills the night.

Then, silence.

Robin turns toward Jessie on Corey.

Corey's face is a deep red, bordering on purple, and a light gurgle escapes his puckering lips. Unable to break Jessie's grip or bend his arms, he manages to reach his holster. Pulling the Smith and Wesson six-shooter revolver from the leather, he aims as best he can and squeezes the trigger.

A loud bang fills the night.

Robin jumps, covering her mouth as a shrill scream escapes.

Jessie's grip loosens. He leans back, turning his attention to the large red stain in the middle of his chest.

Corey takes in a deep and choking breath, pushing Jessie over to the side. Rolling away onto his knees, he gasps and chokes at the rocks. Breaths wheezy and spit stringing down from his lips, he cuts his eyes at Robin.

Jessie puts a hand to his chest, bringing back red-tipped fingers. "You fucking shot me." He marvels at the blood on his fingers.

Corey does his best to stand, fighting against whatever drug they put in his system.

Robin rushes to Jessie's side, hovering a shaking hand over his wound. "No, baby, baby.... Nooo... Ssshhh." She pets him, lip and chin quivering again.

Jessie coughs, and red sprays over her, covering her half-dead mermaid costume. Gargling and choking on his own blood, he soon slips away at Robin's knees.

Corey takes a few fumbling steps backwards.

The crunching stones beneath his feet break the silence, calling Robin's attention to him.

A sudden jolt of adrenaline hits as Corey realizes his mistake in moving.

Robin snarls, getting to her feet with immense speed, and rushes him, fingers curled for the attack. Before he can react, she's on him, forcing him back down. Flinging her fists, she does her best to claw at him, bite him, or punch him.

Corey drops the gun, putting up his arms in defense, and does what he can to grab her. It's no use. Her flails and erratic movements are too unpredictable, and he can't latch on. Keeping his arms up, he glances to his right.

The cold steel of the revolver glints so close yet so far way.

Turning back to her, Corey manages a grip at her waist and pushes her off him. Scrambling, he moves for the gun.

Robin flings herself back onto him, pulling at his pants and legs.

Fingers centimeters away, Corey reaches with all he has.

Robin jerks his pants, pulling him to her a small amount.

Glancing back at her, Corey grits his teeth, lunging, and grabs enough of the grip to pull it to him. Grabbing tight, he swings it around, aiming, and squeezes the trigger.

Robin's head jolts backward, blood and brains spewing over the stones, and her body is flung to the roof behind her.

The rocks roll and crack under her weight, but she doesn't move.

Huffing out, Corey makes himself go into a small coughing fit. Rolling over, he coughs at the stones, taking in deep and raspy breaths. Finding his footing, he stands, eyeing over the scene before him. He holsters his weapon and moves to the edge of the roof. Leaning over, he peers out at the gravel drive, landing on Miku, and jerks his gaze away.

Body splayed out.

Red splattered over the gravel.

Corey does what he can to shake the image from his mind but can't seem to make it go away. Opening his eyes, he ignores her, scanning the area for possible ways to climb down. Roaming the entirety of the massive roof, he finds an old fire escape at the back. After climbing to the ground below, he makes his way down the drive to what looks to be an actual road.

Headlights shine from far off, advancing fast.

Corey moves to the double yellow lines, waving his arms over his head.

The car comes to a tire-squealing halt feet away from him.

Corey rushes to the driver's door, banging on the window.

The woman inside cracks it just a bit, thick Southern voice shaking. "Do you need some help, mister?" She eyes him over, glancing around the night through her windshield.

Corey's voice is hoarse, coming out for the first time since Jessie's hands were on him. "I need to borrow your cell, there's

DEATH INVITES IN GOLD

been an accident about a mile up this drive." He points a shaking finger behind him, clearing his sore throat.

The woman nods, digging through her purse, and pulls out a flip phone with large buttons. "Here." Not taking any chances, she squeezes it through the crack.

Taking it, Corey manages a nod and whispers, "Thank you." Dialing nine, one, one, he waits as the ring fills his ears.

"911, what is your emergency?"

Corey takes in as deep a breath as he can muster, voice cooperating in spurts. "Yes, this is Officer Corey Nash of the Redondo Beach, California, police department. Badge number 987. I'm reporting a series of murders and requesting backup." He pauses, glancing at the woman's wide eyes and gaping mouth.

"Sir, what is your location at this time?"

Corey locks eyes with the woman. "Uh, what road is this?" He points to the asphalt.

The woman blinks a few times, shaking her head, and squeezes the steering wheel. "Oh, uh, uh, um, Highway 322. Between Herrensburg and Mill Creek."

Corey mouths a thank you, moving the mouthpiece upward. "I'm on Highway 322 between Herrensburg and Mill Creek."

"Alright, sir, the police and an ambulance are on their way."

Standing tall, Corey eyes the void between him and the woods on the other side of the highway. "What is your ETA?" He takes in a wheezing breath.

"ETA is twenty minutes. You're quite a ways out there, sir."

Corey sighs, nodding. "Yes, ma'am, that I am." Glancing around at nothing in particular, he closes the phone and shoves it through the cracked window. "Thank you, ma'am." Nodding once, he glances around again, letting out a sigh, and wipes his mouth.

———

MILL CREEK PD three days later

95

Corey sits in an interrogation room not so different from the one he and Nathan shared so many times before.

Only this time, he is sitting cuffed to the table.

The door opens, and an older white-haired cop enters, unlocking the cuffs. "Sorry about all that, you know the drill." He sits across the table, plopping a file down.

Corey rubs his wrists, cocking his head, and lets out a harsh chuckle. "Yea, I know the drill with weekend holds, I feel sure." Shaking his head, he eyes the file.

The cop points at it, pressing that finger into the manilla folder. "We did a little digging, and it didn't take much time or effort." He leans back, crossing his arms. "Well, the girl you say was named Robin is actually Wanda Wilkinson. She was seeing a Dr. Weltzer for social anxiety and the inability to cope with a bodily disfigurement on her face." Sighing, he shrugs, lifting his hand from his arm. "She went to school with the victims, claiming in her sessions that they bullied her about her face." He eyes the table, wiping his mouth.

Corey leans forward. "And the guy? Jessie?" His vinyl-covered seat squeaks under his shifting weight.

The cop cuts his eyes up at him. "Another former patient of the good doctor. One being treated for excessively violent behaviors. One who cheated the system and was allowed in public. With his help, she modified an old high school into that freak show and lured those poor kids." He snarls, pulling an evidence bag from his suit jacket containing a digital recorder. "Her doctor was so mortified by her and Jessie's actions, he waved confidentiality and gave us the recording of her last session with him. I think he felt guilty and somewhat responsible." He removes the recorder, pressing play.

———

The Big Apple, 2016:

A Manhattan office complex:

Wanda leans up from the slick burgundy leather couch and glances over at the man sitting across from her in a matching arm chair. "I bumped into Tyler on the sidewalk here on Broadway on my way to get lunch. He turned to me with a smile and apologized. Didn't even recognize me, the ass. I hadn't seen him in years, and the fact that he didn't remember me enough to recognize me brought me here. All the torment from school came back in a swarm of memories, and so I came straight to you, Dr. Weltzer." She glares at him from the corner of her eye.

Dr. Weltzer nods, putting the bottom of his pen to his pursed lips, and peers at her through thick-rimmed glasses. "I see, I see. What are your coping mechanisms, Wanda? You do remember them, don't you? I know it's been quite a while since you've been triggered." He rests the pen against his chin.

Wanda rises to a sitting position, facing him, and furrows her eyebrows. "Coping mechanisms? I've been seeing you for three years now, and you think those stupid mantras and calming techniques work for me?" Her face contorts as she shakes her head, and her words come out fast and loud. "The only coping mechanism I have is my increasing talent to cover my horrific birthmark." She brushes her light auburn hair from her face, revealing a flawless makeup job. "I spend hundreds of dollars a month to maintain this perfection, and yet I still remain in a constant fear of it being found." She lowers her hair, batting thickly mascaraed eyelashes below perfectly arched drawn-on eyebrows.

Dr. Weltzer nods again, pressing his fingertips together, and points them all at her. "Okay, it seems to me that instead of hiding the blemish, you need to embrace it. Own it. It's a part of you, and you should showcase it." He pauses, clearing his throat, and turns his eyes to the floor. "It's unprofessional of me to say this, but I believe you need to hear it and that it may help." He locks eyes with her. "You're actually quite beautiful despite your insecurity." He grins, resting his hands in his lap, and clears his throat again while looking at the other side of the room. "However, to solve your trigger problem, why don't you arrange a meeting with the group? Maybe then, you can all get past the old high-school drama and actually get to know each other for real. Who knows, maybe they're different now." He shrugs, crossing his legs.

She locks eyes with him. "You know, I've actually thought about that. I want to see what sort of adults they turned out to be." She flits an uneasy grin his way. "I have high hopes they've changed, but for the most part I feel as though they're still the same little shits they used to be." She chews her bottom lip, turning her eyes to the floor.

The man shrugs, tugging at the ends of his sweater's sleeves. "I still suggest a meeting of sorts. Make them wish they'd never made fun of you by forcing them to face the blemish head on, and show them you no longer allow the fear of embarrassment or taunting to control you. Show them how much you've grown and how the blemish hasn't taken anything from you." He smiles, putting his hands behind his back.

Wanda's eyes widen, lips parting a bit, and she nods with a slight grin. "Force them to see it, get them back for all the years of torment." Her grin grows to a wide smile. "Yes." The smile overtakes her face. "That's what I'll do. Thank you, Dr. Weltzer." She stands, extending a hand.

Dr. Weltzer stands, smoothing out his sweater, and clears his throat. "You do know I'm suggesting a well-lit and public area, correct? I don't want you doing anything rash." He arches an eyebrow, tilting his head towards her, and glares as he clasps her hand.

Wanda nods several times. "Oh, yes, well-lit, public, got it." Shaking his hand as many times as she nodded, she lets go, grabbing her purse, and heads to her car.

———

REDONDO BEACH, CALIFORNIA, THREE WEEKS LATER:

RBPD

Corey sits at his desk, staring at the computer screen.

One of the clerks steps up to his desk, dropping a manilla envelope on top of his keyboard. "Some weird old man dropped this off for you." Arching an eyebrow, he shrugs, shaking his head, and walks off.

Corey furrows his eyebrows, straightening the metal tabs, and flips up the fold. Dipping his fingers inside, he pulls out a thin stack of papers.

The page on top has a simple message:

To the lucky winner of my golden invitation, you are now the soul owner of my property, possessions, and monetary value. All explained here within the enclosed documents.

Sifting through the other pages, Corey finds the deed to the school. A deed to her house. A last will and testament. And banking information. Peering into the bottom of the envelope, he turns it over and watches a set of keys fall on his desk. Flipping over the attached tag, he reads the small script.

'Safety deposit box #678.'

Glancing around the precinct, Corey puts everything back.

That weekend, Corey packs up his apartment, heading for a new start.

Dear reader,

We hope you enjoyed reading *Death Invites in Gold*. Please take a moment to leave a review, even if it's a short one. Your opinion is important to us.

Discover more books by Rachel Bross at https://www.nextchapter.pub/authors/rachel-bross

Want to know when one of our books is free or discounted? Join the newsletter at http://eepurl.com/bqqB3H

Best regards,

Rachel Bross and the Next Chapter Team

Printed in Great Britain
by Amazon

82533148R00062